PRAISE FOR

The Foreigners

"Swann, an American who has lived in Buenos Aires for the past decade, vividly evokes the city and its lively, diverse, and conflicted social landscape, from the denizens of posh hotels to the unfortunate poor living in the city's slums. . . . Seductively hard to put down."
—*The Boston Globe*

"The three women in Maxine Swann's *The Foreigners* hope to leave their worries behind by plunging into the wild glamour of Buenos Aires, but find even greater surprises when they stumble into the recesses of their own lives."
—*W Magazine*

"Post-crash Buenos Aires is the noirish setting of Maxine Swann's *The Foreigners*, in which an untethered American divorcée dabbles in increasingly risky funny games with the help of a local provocateuse."
—*Vogue*

"The city of Buenos Aires dazzles in this novel about three women who find sex, adventure, and more sex in the Paris of South America."
—*O, The Oprah Magazine*

"Enticing."
—*San Francisco Chronicle*

"With lyricism and observational skill that recalls early Joan Didion, Swann brings Buenos Aires to life." —*Publishers Weekly*

continued . . .

"Atmospheric, evocative literary fiction that ruminates on what it means and how it feels to be foreign." —*Booklist*

"Beautifully written, sensual, and seductive." —*Kirkus Reviews*

PRAISE FOR *FLOWER CHILDREN*
A *People* Magazine Critic's Choice

"A small gem of a novel . . . keenly observed."
—*The New York Times*

"Spellbinding . . . Swann evokes the wonder of childhood . . . with an almost hallucinatory precision." —*Vogue*

"A work of stunning lyricism and intense originality. It tells a story many of us have been waiting to hear: what happened to those children brought up in the wake of the dream of the sixties."
—Mary Gordon, author of *Pearl*

"I didn't want this book to end. It is mesmerizing."
—Eliza Minot, author of *The Brambles*

"Full of the visceral pleasures and anxieties of childhood."
—*Los Angeles Times Book Review*

"Hypnotic . . . Swann's writing is mesmerizing . . . readers won't soon forget the portraits of flower children struggling to bloom in a very different world from the one in which they were first planted." —*People*

Also by Maxine Swann

Flower Children

Serious Girls

the Foreigners

Maxine Swann

RIVERHEAD BOOKS
New York

RIVERHEAD BOOKS
Published by the Penguin Group
Penguin Group (USA) Inc.
375 Hudson Street, New York, New York 10014, USA

Penguin Group (Canada), 90 Eglinton Avenue East, Suite 700, Toronto, Ontario M4P 2Y3, Canada
(a division of Pearson Penguin Canada Inc.) • Penguin Books Ltd., 80 Strand, London WC2R 0RL,
England • Penguin Group Ireland, 25 St. Stephen's Green, Dublin 2, Ireland (a division of Penguin
Books Ltd.) • Penguin Group (Australia), 250 Camberwell Road, Camberwell, Victoria 3124, Australia
(a division of Pearson Australia Group Pty. Ltd.) • Penguin Books India Pvt. Ltd., 11 Community
Centre, Panchsheel Park, New Delhi—110 017, India • Penguin Group (NZ), 67 Apollo Drive,
Rosedale, Auckland 0632, New Zealand (a division of Pearson New Zealand Ltd.) • Penguin Books
(South Africa) (Pty.) Ltd., 24 Sturdee Avenue, Rosebank, Johannesburg 2196, South Africa

Penguin Books Ltd., Registered Offices: 80 Strand, London WC2R 0RL, England

This is a work of fiction. Names, characters, places, and incidents either are the product of the author's
imagination or are used fictitiously, and any resemblance to actual persons, living or dead, business
establishments, events, or locales is entirely coincidental. The publisher does not have any control over
and does not assume any responsibility for author or third-party websites or their content.

First Riverhead hardcover edition: August 2011
First Riverhead trade paperback edition: August 2012
Riverhead trade paperback ISBN: 978-1-59448-581-7

The Library of Congress has catalogued the Riverhead hardcover edition as follows:

Swann, Maxine.
The foreigners / Maxine Swann.
p.   cm.
ISBN 978-1-59448-830-6
1. Self-realization in women—Fiction.   2. Buenos Aires (Argentina)—Fiction.   I. Title.
PS3619.W356F67   2011   2011009413
813'.6—dc22

PRINTED IN THE UNITED STATES OF AMERICA

10 9 8 7 6 5 4 3 2 1

to P

Part I

one

The amount of pollen that comes in on travelers' sleeves is vastly disproportionate to the number of species that hold. However, once an invasive species takes root, it can become voracious. An apparently innocent figure can topple whole ecosystems. Consider, for example, the rosy wolf snail of the southeastern United States. Or the case of the *Iris pseudacorus* currently taking over the Argentine wetlands, threatening to annihilate the habitat of the Curve-billed Reedhaunter and the Asian privet.

The foreigners in Buenos Aires come, searching as they always were, for a kind of utopia, though the definition of "utopia" varies. They fall into categories. There are the South American neighbors, Bolivians, Paraguayans, Peruvians, who come to work as maids, construction and agricultural workers and send the money home. The Belarusians come because there is an accord with their country, still now, papers delivered unquestionably. There are, apparently—it has not only been rumored but confirmed—whole communities of Africans. They are being taught the language so as to insert themselves. But where they are inserted remains a mystery. They are never seen. A black-skinned person on the street is an anomaly. Everyone, however furtively, turns and stares.

Then there is the other type of foreigner, coming out of curiosity, for a lark, backpackers, tango dancers, often the lark-seeking obscuring deeper, more complicated, half-conscious reasons, escape from overdetermined social trajectories, troubled families, marriages or lack of prospects. This group, in turn, bifurcates. The tango dancers conglomerate among themselves, into bigger and bigger masses. Friendships are light, turnover expected. The tango life is exigent, starting at two, three in the morning. You're out until dawn, sleep through the mornings, then pick up some odd jobs in the late afternoon hours until the night begins again. In general, this crowd isn't picky, nor that interested in money. Their lives are centered around one goal.

The motives of the other group are more complex. They arrive, Europeans, in the new world. "I've discovered the continent inhabited by more peoples and animals than our Europe or Asia or Africa itself, and I've found that the air here is more temperate and sweet than in any other part of the world we know," wrote Vespuccio in 1507. "I hereby name it Mundus Novus." The new world today seems to hold all the promise it ever did, exotic fauna and flora, potential for exploitation. Like the Belarusians and the Asians, these foreigners are taking their chances, only in a different tier and what they're after is more fleeting—glamour, big wealth, upper-class status, things they can't find at home, because they don't make the grade. But in Argentina it's different. No matter what their origins, by virtue of being European or American, as long as they're basically decently physically assembled, they're immediately endowed with a certain sheen, upper class unless proven otherwise, instead of the reverse. In the case of ugliness, of course, as always, other strategies must be sought. They learn to speak Spanish sufferingly well, with smatterings of other languages slipped in—among upper-class Argentines this is par for the course.

Though the potential for circulation is one of the great virtues of Buenos Aires, revolving city events, everyone goes, this particular group is interested in exclusivity. While at the end of the nineteenth century the places to be seen among the Argentine aristocracy were balls, dog walks, church masses, and above all the promenades of Palermo—on Thursdays and Sunday afternoons, four lines of cars would drive back and forth along the three blocks of what is now Sarmiento Avenue—and then later in the 1920s, the river islands of Tigre, where significant yachts would cross each other on the tranquil muddy waters, now the viewing places, as this particular breed of foreigner soon assesses, are museum openings, opera galas and cocktail parties. They can soon be seen at all the requisite events, typing contacts into their shiny cell phones.

For all its supposed glamour, the milieu ages you. Even the younger women look older than they are. The foreigners, starry-eyed, don't realize this yet. They still can't get over having maids. They marvel secretly to themselves that they would ever have a maid, someone to fold and arrange their clothes, they who grew up the way they did, although here too there's a cultural conundrum—every basic middle-class Argentine household has a maid. But they soon not only behave as if, but begin to feel that, they could never live without one. Still, their two main concerns are the concerns of most of us, commerce and love.

As for me, I arrived in Buenos Aires in 2002 in a peculiar state. I was thirty-five.

My marriage of nine years had dissolved the year before. Around the same time, I'd switched jobs. My husband had been a theater director. When I met him, I'd started working in stage design, but I now found myself disenchanted with that world. We lived in Seattle, where I had grown up. While looking around for a different line of work, I signed on as the assistant to a botanist I met at a dinner party, as an intermediate step. Still, I had yet to get my bearings. It wasn't that I'd been happy or unhappy with my husband. But the devotion I'd felt for him had been entirely absorbing.

My parents, divorced themselves, however amicably, were concerned. My father, a lawyer, had friends of his take care of my divorce paperwork. My mother, a social worker, suggested counseling. I did go to see a counselor; our conversations were interesting, yet they did nothing to prevent that in January of the year following my separation, I started fainting inexplicably. It would begin in my ears, sounds seeming to come from far away, then my vision would go into high-contrast mode, the brights blinding and the darks almost invisible for being so black. Once I had fainted a few times, and I knew what these signals meant, I could sometimes lie down in time to keep myself from going under. When I did pass out, it would seem like an eternity. Sometimes, I would shake as if I was going into convulsions or pee myself. One day, it happened on the street in Seattle. The next thing I knew I was down on the pavement throwing up like crazy, surrounded by firemen and paramedics. That time, I had gone so far under, I really felt that I had died and I heard this drumbeat filling my head getting slower and slower (the nurse said later that it was my heart), until everything came rushing back again with ice-cold liquid filling my veins from the IVs they'd stuck in me (it was winter and the stuff was cold from being in the ambulance). I was a mess, covered in vomit, pee and poo everywhere, but I actually felt exhilarated when I woke up. Riding in the ambulance to the hospital, I remembered being in Spain as a college student and imagined myself as one of those huge religious sculptures they carry in processions.

They kept me in the hospital for almost a week and did a million tests, blood tests and epilepsy tests, tests of my heart, an MRI of my brain, another test where they attached electrical probes to my head and sent shocks to different parts of my body. But it was finally concluded from the tests and repeated tests that there was nothing organically wrong with me. The head doctor came into my room one day on the neurology ward to report this and say that they could find no further justification for keeping me there.

Later that afternoon, following a visit from my mother, my friend Brian stopped by.

"You know what you should do?" he said, after hearing the news. "Take a trip."

"A trip?" I asked, vaguely surprised. I had traveled with my husband to Portugal, Morocco and Greece but, apart from that semester in college when I'd lived in Barcelona, I'd never gone anywhere on my own.

"Yeah, anywhere. Just go somewhere. I know," he said. "I'm on this board now. I can arrange for you to get a grant. But it would have to be in urban studies." That was his field.

"Oh, God."

"Don't worry. It doesn't matter if you do it. The point is to get you some money to go somewhere. Let's see. You speak Spanish, right? Yeah, I think I can work it out."

This was how I found myself one month later in the airport on my way to Buenos Aires with a grant to study the public water-works of the city. They say that every hospitalization is a journey. They also say that when people enter the hospital, they leave part of themselves outside. Maybe the conjunction of these two ele-ments explains the estrangement you feel on leaving. Part of you has taken a journey, of which the other part is ignorant. Part of you returns, reencounters the part you left outside. The two of you do what you can to proceed. It was in this state of estrangement that I set out.

My stint in the hospital had made it clear how little is actu-ally known by doctors, by ourselves, about the human condition. "We're all tapping along in the dark," as one neurologist who exam-ined me put it. In the airport, waiting for my plane to board, I was leafing through a magazine when I glanced up and caught a glimpse of what looked like the head doctor from the hospital. He was standing in profile, about ten yards away. Then he turned and approached the set of seats where I was. Now I could see, it was definitely him. He was small, with green eyes set somewhat close. I had never seen him out of his hospital gown. I immediately had the reflex to hide, as if I was doing something wrong, as if, if he saw me, I'd be forbidden to leave. While before I'd felt somewhat baffled by my actions, suddenly it seemed quite imperative that I leave. I ducked out of sight, put on some new sunglasses I'd bought whose lenses were especially, even too, dark. The trip took on an air of the forbidden. Although I hadn't been aware of it until this moment, I seemed to be living it as a renegade expedition.

My first days in Buenos Aires were sufficiently disorienting to absorb my full attention. It was April, autumn, and the city seemed to have a lugubrious air. All the stereotypical melancholic idea was there, pervasive, stinking like the waters in the La Boca zone, and this even more so because of the recent economic crash. My own financial situation was steady for the moment—along with the grant money, I had some savings, and since the peso had been devalued, everything was cheap. I was staying in the house of a woman in her late sixties named Cecilia until I got my bearings, also an arrangement made by Brian.

The apartment was on the second floor and, as I would later learn, like all middle- and upper-class Buenos Aires apartments, had a balcony with plants. Outside on the street, the very loud buses went by. The plants fluttered. The tiny china plates on gold hooks on the walls quivered. The polished dining room table was never used. On the sideboard was a large crystal liquor container surrounded by crystal glasses. The furniture, Cecilia liked to say, was French. The upholstered couches and chairs, salmon pink, were covered in plastic so as not to get stained by people who never came. When you sat there in warm weather, the plastic stuck to your legs. There were life-size portrait photographs of Cecilia's two children receiving communion. The rooms were kept ready, waiting for the children, someone, but no one ever came.

In the meantime, Cecilia, like many others, had had all access to her savings blocked by the recent bank debacle. The money was floating in some unidentified place, who knew if ever to be seen again, which meant that she either had to sell her apartment and move to a smaller, humbler place or go out and get a job. The only thing she had was her apartment. She had decided to get a job and worked now in a travel agency, long hours, five days a week.

It seemed to me that there was in this woman's life a shadowy flickering of my own, hopes suspended, though her case, of course, was more extreme. Still the resemblance would sometimes make me feel that I was drowning and I'd wake up in the night in an appalling state, feverish, with the sensation that a substance was flooding my lungs. Lying there, I'd picture the streets of Buenos Aires flooded with dark water, up, up over my head. I'd see Cecilia trying to make her way home from work, battling against the current, now well past her thighs. Another time, on waking, I had the distinct impression that a being was holding me from behind, a sort of fiend, clutching me tight, which later struck me as an almost miraculous embodiment of some allegorical idea of death. The life-size photographic figures of the absent children would dance before my eyes. Or else I'd dream of crowds.

An aspect of the city, especially prevalent at the moment, was protesting crowds. They could be found on any given day. All you had to do was step out into the street and listen. They were often around the Pink House, the residence of the president, but would also move through the streets. I found myself gravitating toward them. People would be milling around in one location, sometimes banging pots and pans. Occasionally the crowd would erupt, the police arriving, everyone running. But it was strange because, while for me the crowds during the day offered solace—I would find myself drawn toward them and enclosed there—in my nightmare visions, they did not. The crowds in my mind took the form of insects, reptilian animals, they were crawling over me, invading my bed, or simply a repeated pattern, of light, squirmy shapes, seething, retreating, coming forward again.

Apart from these visions, there was nothing particularly notable about my loneliness, or rather it was all that there was, all that was there. Go back? That was not an option either. Utopia has been defined for many as not what you go toward but what you get away from, utopia because it's not the old life. No matter what it offered, Buenos Aires was in that sense utopia for me.

I did have enough lucidity to realize that my living situation was degrading my outlook. Cecilia, despite her dire straits, refused to accept any payment for the room I was using. This, combined with the bizarre visions the apartment was provoking in my mind, led me to set about looking for a place. From the newspaper I contacted a real estate agency and was assigned to an agent named Olga.

Olga was Bolivian and had a face that looked like it had been carved onto a coin, large olive-colored eyes with visible lids, a straight nose, her long light brown hair tinged with gold pulled back in a ponytail tight from her face. She took me around in taxis, was quick and efficient and her English was good.

"Argentines say this is the widest avenue in the world," Olga said as we crossed the 9 de Julio. "But Argentines say a lot of things, like that they invented the artificial heart."

The taxi driver turned and said something to her. She shot back a long line of heated invectives that I couldn't catch.

"See," she said, "he hears my accent and thinks because I'm Bolivian he can say anything to me. They're all like that."

"Who?"

"Argentines. They think they're better than the rest of us."

The taxi driver laughed, enjoying her spitfire behavior.

As we drove around, she told me that she was married but didn't live with her husband anymore, though they almost always had dinner together. "No, no," she said, "he's not someone you live with." She had a son, twenty years old now. She was a business-woman. That was her identity and she was proud of it. "My son always gives me presents for a businesswoman, pens, leather cases."

I liked Olga but one after another of the apartments she took me to gave me an appalling sense of suffocation. They were fluffy white boxes of varying sizes, all in the central area, Barrio Norte and downtown. Even the apartments with more than one room felt close and small, the appliances brand new, the floorboards painted.

Our search went on for a week or so.

"There's a last apartment if you actually want to see it," Olga said one day. "I don't like the place at all. I hate old buildings. I hate everything old. I want everything to be new, new, new."

We crossed the 9 de Julio again and stopped in front of a build-ing with a large door, incongruous with all the doors around, on Carlos Pellegrini Street.

"I don't like this place," Olga said again as we stepped inside, both pressing open the heavy door.

There was a wide passageway with a tiled floor. The far wall didn't go all the way up to the ceiling, leaving an open-air space. Later, I saw that the hallways on all the floors were like this, partly open to the air. Flowers and leaves would fall inside. It would rain on the floor.

"This place is abandoned," Olga said. "I never see anyone here."

We walked up the wide dim staircase to the second floor. The door of the apartment resisted, as if it hadn't been opened for a while. Inside, the place had a kept, cut-off air. It was silent. Vines lined the windows outside. There was a chaise lounge covered in worn purple velvet. You felt in your own world, cut off from the rest.

"This place gives me the creeps," Olga said.

But there was something about it I liked.

"I'll take it," I said.

The Polish writer Witold Gombrowicz, exiled in Buenos Aires because of World War II, and then staying on, wrote about the seediness of the ports. In passages of his diaries, where the sense suddenly darkens, blurs, we enter a vacuum, he talks about his activity in the ports, these meetings with young men. It's the youth of Buenos Aires that intrigued him, the beautiful youth. He describes his own rejuvenation there, culminating in a moment when, vertiginous in the company of young people, he goes off to the bathroom and, looking in the mirror, sees the lines all over his face and, for the first time really, understands that he's old.

Now the ports, as they once were, are gone. Instead in that spot there's an artificial city under construction, largely the work of Russian developers, flashy hotels, apartment complexes, illuminated patches of grass. To get back to the city from the ports you have to cross a wasteland, on the other side of which lies what is known as "downtown."

The streets of downtown, bustling during the day, are abandoned at night as if they hadn't been inhabited for years. Your footsteps sound against them. What's odd is that unlike in the rest of the city, here there's no green. Everywhere else the streets are lined with trees, the balconies of the apartments are deluged with plants, green above and green below. Often, as you're walking, water drips down on your head from plants that have just been watered above. Then there are the trees that drip naturally, the tipa. At certain times of the year, due to the parasite *Cephisus siccifolius*, which sucks the sap from the tree and excretes it in the form of a sugary liquid, the passerby, walking under, feels specks of water, like very light rain. Flamboyant, the Buenos Aires trees bloom not once but at several seasons. The jacaranda tree has pale purple blossoms that fall off long before they're withered, littering the ground with pale purple trumpets; the palo borracho has pink blossoms, hand-size, the whole tree flames up with them; the small yellow flowers on the tipa trees give off a dizzying smell.

All the green downtown is collected in the Plaza San Martín. Against the trees here, so tall, a human is an insect. A lawn slopes down to the main avenue. Just beyond is the bus station, Retiro, also known as a site for seedy activity (don't, you're told, go there at night, unless you're looking for seedy activity, in which case, do), and the port beyond. On the lawn that falls down from the Plaza San Martín, people lie out to sunbathe or sleep, exhausted in the middle of the workday. You can find men in business suits, women in stockings, eyes closed, passed out. People come here to kiss. In the evenings, in the darker spots, near where there are trees, you could practically make love, and people do. You think at first that everyone in Buenos Aires is in love. Then you realize that, in fact, many people live with their parents until much later in life, through their thirties, into their forties even. This is even more the case after the crash, when people who did have their own apartments gave them up and moved back home. So of course everyone's always making out everywhere. They have nowhere else to go. Unless they can afford a hotel room. The city is full of these. You can find one on nearly every corner. You pay for two hours. (In Brazil, in these same hotels, you pay for three hours, a difference that has given rise to much speculation.) The rooms are often decorated with themes: ancient Greece, New York, the jungle room. There's a plastic sheet to protect the mattress.

When night comes, the Buenos Aires streets are alive with people who live on the periphery in slums and come in in dilapidated vehicles or horse-drawn wooden carts to sift through garbage. They collect the recyclables and bring them back to a warehouse where they're sorted. They're paid a piddling amount for all that labor, which is orchestrated through a corruption ring, the proceeds from which barely get them through the day, until evening comes and they go out again. In certain neighborhoods, there are no vestiges of this underlife during the day. The sun shines down on the Parisian-style buildings—the sun nearly always shines in Buenos Aires—and the glinting breezes blow up from the river, only to be interrupted occasionally by an abrupt downpour out of the blue, thundering ropes of rain that flood all the streets—the drainage system needs attention—and then just as abruptly cease, leaving the streets still flooded and, in certain neighborhoods where rents are cheaper for this very reason, even the houses flooded, all the first floors. Old women, unable to get from their places of work to the bus stop, can be seen wading knee-high against the current. Cars make turns on flooded corners, the water off the wheels spraying up in swaths, then pummeling down on storefront windows. Very, very slowly, the water goes down. When will they refurbish the drains? Surely not now, not for a while.

My new apartment was quiet. There were black-and-white tiles in the hallway. Every now and then a winged cockroach flew through the kitchen. The owner, Olga had told me, had gone to Europe and disappeared. Her brother rented the place out for her now. In the living room was a vine that wanted to creep in the window. "If you let it, you'll have ants," Olga said. I decided to let it for the moment.

"Are you sure you're going to be all right?" Olga asked on leaving me the day I moved in. I reassured her.

The windows looked out on an abandoned back garden. No one ever went there. To one side was the white wall of the adjacent building. When it rained, water ran down the wall. I would sit there on the chaise lounge staring at the sheen of water for hours.

It was a mammoth building. There was no one in the halls. Sometimes, rarely, I'd hear a key turning. Another time, from the hallway, I heard the sounds of people making love in a somewhat brutal fashion. But the walls were thick. Once I was inside my apartment, I listened again and heard nothing.

I had paid Olga six months in advance. When the phone rang, it would startle me. It was always a wrong number. I felt as if, apart from Olga, nobody knew I was here.

In one of the books Brian had given me, I'd read about nineteenth-century urban plans to build parks or "green lungs" all over Buenos Aires, to ward off the infestations of tuberculosis. The idea was that the disease festered in the tiny cramped quarters with no ventilation where crowds of people lived on top of one another. The green lungs would allow these people open-air spaces where they could escape from their homes and come to sit and breathe. Now it seemed that instead of momentary refuges, people had just settled directly in the parks or plazas. This was new, Olga had told me. The year before there had hardly been a homeless person on the street. Now the square outside my building was full of people huddled, individuals, whole families, camped out, it seemed, permanently, and then right here this empty building.

Around the corner from my house was a church. At Mass hours, especially in the evening, people would be pressing in at the doorway, spilling out, couples, families, teenagers in their coolest clothes casting sidelong glances. One night, post-Mass, I saw a small group gathered on the church steps with baskets of food. I asked what they were doing and a woman, slightly cross-eyed, told me they were going around to feed the homeless. I asked if I could join them and she agreed, taking my hand in hers. It turned out to be an odd venture. As we moved around the streets from one cluster of homeless people to the next, the cross-eyed woman wouldn't let go of my hand. If I dropped hers, she'd find a way to sidle over to me and pick mine up again. Not being able to bear this anymore, I finally broke away and hurried down a side street on my own.

On another corner was a small *parrilla,* or classic Argentine barbecue restaurant, where I'd go sometimes for a meal. I'd sit against the wall by the window. The waiter, a man who must have been in his fifties, with a long face and droopy eyes that showed the lower part of his eyeballs, called me "daughter," as they sometimes did here. I'd wait for him to call me "daughter" when he was asking for my order or afterward, when he was bringing me the food. It was as if the food, the atmosphere were secondary. I'd come to hear him say that.

At the end of the block was a *locutorio.* The *locutorio,* I'd quickly grasped, was an Argentine institution, a public place lined with phone booths and computers where you could go to write an e-mail or make a call. They were always bustling. Even the cell phone culture hadn't stymied them. You could sit down in the booths. Often there was a mirror. Women, as they were talking, fixed their makeup and hair. People who'd lost their offices during the crash ran their businesses from here, students without computers shacked up to write their papers. Kids sat in rows playing video games. Of course, there were undoubtedly all kinds of illicit things occurring there as well, in the privacy of telephone booths and computer screens. I would go every few days and read my e-mails, from friends, from my mother, from my ex-boss, the botanist. But I rarely lingered. My other life seemed, in all ways, far away.

Thinking it would be good if I met some people, I decided to put up signs at the university offering English classes. The Philosophy and Letters branch, previously a factory building, was far from the center of the city. I went there one afternoon. The entranceway was low and dim. The walls, ceiling to floor, even along the stairs, were papered with bulletins, calls for meetings, political tracts, torn off, recovered, torn again, giving the impression of an entire interior plastered with papier mâché. In the bathrooms, there were no toilet seats and no paper. Rather than carrying books around, the students for the most part carried photocopies. Later, I would learn that this was because books were expensive. I wandered around on the different floors, looking in doorways and posting my own signs.

In the afternoons, I walked. I always took the same route, down the hill to the big avenue. Along the avenue, there were brilliant green patches, grassy spots with trees. Thick pods from the palo borracho trees burst and spread tufts of cotton all over the ground. There were several statues I liked, one of a girl in rough stone, nearly featureless but with curves, sitting and leaning to the side, propping herself up with her hand, another of a faun. He was behind her, up on his hind legs. One night, he appeared in my dream. "I want to suck your armpit," he said. I walked here almost every day, but then, as sometimes happened when I had nothing to do, I walked on endlessly for hours.

I circled outward into neighborhoods I didn't know, the pale buildings, dark doorways, the plazas with dogs loitering, a fountain not working but half filled with copper-colored rainwater, the clanking buses hurtling by. I'd lose my way completely in streets whose names I didn't know. The whole sky was light. The shadows looked blacker here than anywhere I remembered. I would get walking and wouldn't stop. In the wide dark doorway of a garage a man stood in the center cutting up meat.

As I said, there were often crowds. Sometimes I skirted them, looked and skirted. One time I got caught up. Something happened. We were out in front of the government building. There were policemen with plastic shields, a helicopter overhead. The crowd started to panic, ran. One guy with his pants down was running right toward me. He must have been caught off-guard peeing. I ran too. We were in a square, dodging statues. My heart was racing. There was exhilaration mixed with the fear. People were scrambling, touching, in a way that would have been impossible under any other circumstance. In one moment, we were all rubbing against each other and the next we were dispersed. I found myself spiraling off, into a new neighborhood. I slowed down, catching my breath.

The Jardín Botánico was crawling with cats, hundreds and hundreds of them. They crept over everything, collected, preened.

The city would abruptly change the subject. I had felt this from the start. You were walking along a smooth Palermo street lined with bars and shops and would suddenly stumble into a wasteland, grass and dirt. Or you looked through a doorway into a huge empty hole. It was an unfinished city, but not only that. It seemed interminable, an interminable job. This was also what I liked.

two

I went to make tea one morning, only to realize that the faucet was dry. I had no water. I called Olga, but was told by her son that she was in New York, on a trip. She loved New York. It was her dream, she had told me, to live there—there people treated you well. I looked for the owner's brother's number. I called and left a message. No response. Having the vaguest understanding of how these things work, I decided to take a look up on the roof. I had a dim memory of a nighttime Seattle rooftop and a water tank there.

I didn't take the elevator but the stairs. I climbed, floor after empty floor. On the fourth floor, there was the sound of a key and then a man standing there, black hair cut close, wearing a raincoat. He seemed as surprised to see me as I was to see him. I nodded, kept climbing. The stairs gave me confidence, as opposed to the elevator. I heard a burst of classical music—it sounded like a Mahler symphony—coming from below just as I reached the next floor.

After the sixth floor, there was a last, smaller flight of stairs, then a small door leading, as I'd suspected, to the rooftop. It was a clear bright day, a bit cool. I walked out across the roof. There was indeed what looked like a water tank up on a ledge. It sounded like water was running into it right at that moment. I climbed up on the ledge to peer inside. The lid was attached to the tank with wire, only letting me lift it a little bit. But I was right, it was low but fill-ing. The water inside looked dark and wavy. Below the tank was a round, black shape that could have been a pump.

I climbed back down from the ledge. Already while up there, I had felt something. Now I saw what it was. There was a guy looking out over the edge of the rooftop, his back to me. Then he turned and looked over his shoulder. He'd seen me too.

He wore sneakers and corduroys and a shirt with green, red and white stripes, dressed like a kid. He had blondish curls and a mournful expression at odds with his youth. "Hi," I said.

"Hi," he answered from his distance.

I wasn't sure whether to stay or turn away.

"I never see anyone up here," he said.

"I never come up here. This is my first time." I paused. "I came because I don't have any water."

"You live in this building?" he asked.

"Yeah, I'm renting. Do you?"

"No, no, I just have client meetings here sometimes." He looked tired, but like a child would look tired, not the actual worn tiredness of an adult. His skin was rosy and gold.

"Really? That's funny. I never see anyone."

"Yeah, we, my firm, rents a place. So that sucks anyway that you don't have water."

"I know. Especially since I don't know who to call. There isn't like a super, is there?"

He shrugged, a helpless face. "I never see anyone."

"I just don't know anything about how water works, like why it would get shut off," I said. "On the other hand, it seems like there's been some activity. That tank there's filling. And here there's water, or was water, on the ground."

I pointed to a wide stain of water on the rooftop, not a puddle because it was sunken in, but a stain.

By now he'd approached me. He also looked down at the stain, then, looking up, followed it over to the end of a hose. I went with him and, together, following the hose, we came to where it was attached to one side of a pipe. At the point of attachment was a spigot. We turned it on. Nothing happened. Then a little water trickled out of the hose.

We turned it off again.

"You have no water whatsoever?" he asked.

"None."

"Hmm. But there's water in the tank?"

"Yeah, it's filling now."

He stood there, thinking. "I don't know anything about any of this either. But there's someone I know who could help us. I'd have to make a call."

"Would you?" I asked.

"Sure, but my cell phone's out of juice."

"You can call from downstairs," I said.

"I'm Gabriel, by the way," he said. I put out my hand. He looked surprised and shook it. "Where are you from?" he asked.

"The States."

"Oh, really? We can speak English if you like," he said. "I could try. The terrible thing is I can't make jokes in English." He smiled.

When he smiled, his nose wrinkled up and his teeth showed suddenly, altering his face completely. He looked like a demon, as if there were a demon inside him peeking out its head. Then the smile disappeared just as quickly and the serene mournful expression settled on his face again. He had shadows under his eyes, like the shadows children have.

We entered my apartment. "Oh, wow, this is a weird place," he said. He was walking down the checkered hall. "Cool. Weird." We circled through the kitchen—I checked the water again, just in the off shot—then went into the living room.

"Here, the phone's here," I said.

"This is a guy I know, not that well, he's a client, a plumber and an electrician. He can tell us."

He called the guy, whose name was Hugo.

I went back into the kitchen and fiddled with the faucet.

Gabriel got off the phone. "Okay, he says first to check the tank—you did that—and then to check all the valves, here in the apartment and up on the roof. They have to be open, which means to the left counterclockwise." We went around the apartment, looking. I found two valves in the bathroom, another in the kitchen below the sink, all apparently open.

"Okay, now let's check up on the roof," Gabriel said. This time we took the elevator.

"Do you give English classes?" he asked.

"Yeah," I said. "Actually, I'm just starting."

"Maybe I'll take English classes from you."

"Really? Great. Why do you want to learn English?" I asked.

He switched to English hesitantly, moving his hands. "For work, for my work," he said.

We were on the roof again, walking across it. The stain looked smaller, as if it had dried somewhat in the sun.

"What do you do?"

He returned to Spanish. "Well, I was studying medicine, to be a doctor, but then when the crash came, I had to stop and find a job. I've been mostly working as a messenger, you know, for a company that delivers things. They give you one of those little bikes." We had arrived at the water tank. "Okay, now Hugo said there should be a valve around here, just below by the pump."

I climbed up on the ledge of the water tank again. It was still filling, I could hear. Below on the pipe that led to the pump was a valve of a different kind, like a lever. It was up, vertical. I put it down, horizontal, and waited. But you couldn't really tell if anything was happening.

I looked at Gabriel and shrugged.

"I guess we just have to go check downstairs again," he said.

We crossed the stain again and headed for the door.

Back in the apartment, I turned on the water in the sink. Nothing.

"Let me call Hugo again."

I began to feel that I'd never have water again. I heard him talking on the phone. "Okay . . . Yeah . . . Yeah . . . There's a hose coming out of the pipe. Yeah, there is . . . Okay . . . Yeah."

He got off the phone. "Let's go back up. He says that what we did is right, to put that valve horizontal. The other thing is there

26

may be air in the pipes. He says we have to go up and open that hose and let the water run out."

We left the apartment again and took the elevator up.

"Oh, yeah, that's what I was saying," Gabriel said. "What I was actually thinking was that I could use English for my other work."

"What's your other work?" I asked.

"As a 'gigolo.' 'Gigolo,' right?" He said the word in English.

"'Gigolo'?" I wasn't sure I'd heard him right.

"Yeah." He looked at me and laughed. "It's something very new."

"Wait, what do you mean, 'gigolo' like prostitute?"

He nodded.

We crossed to where the hose was and he opened the valve. A little bit of water came out.

"I think it will increase appeal, if I speak English. Some clients are foreign."

I was trying to understand. "This is with men?" I asked. "Your clients are men?"

"Yeah, men. I love men. That's the terrible thing."

A moment later, the hose sputtered, jerked and then the water came streaming out. It darkened the roof where the stain was, spreading liberally to form a little pool.

"We have to let it run," Gabriel said. We watched it together. "Yeah, the gigolo is good. The gigolo works," he said.

I felt a bit shy about discussing this subject with a stranger, but I also had a lot of questions. "Do you do it for the money?" I asked.

"No, no, it's not really for the money, though the money's great. Plus you get benefits, like free dinners. The other day I got a new

CD, the Tori Amos one. But it's more than that. It makes me feel better. When I'm doing it, I feel good, very confident."

"Why?"

"I don't know. I guess the beautiful thing is that it annihilates the whole problem of desire."

"It does?" I felt confused.

"Yeah, it's perfect. Oh, it's beautiful. It's desire that's painful, very, very painful. This way you can have sex without suffering all that pain."

We turned the hose off.

"And the clients you see here are which clients?"

"The prostitute ones. It's a friend of mine's uncle's place. I don't have to pay, that's why."

"Is Hugo a john?"

"Yeah, yeah, he is, actually."

As he was talking, we headed back downstairs. Once inside the apartment, I checked the water. It jerked, spurted and then came out smoothly.

"Yea!" Gabriel said.

He turned to me. "What about you? What are you doing here?" he asked.

I told him about my divorce and how I'd started fainting. It seemed like intimate information, but not so intimate after what he'd told me.

"Did they check for epilepsy?" he asked.

"Yeah, I was in the hospital, they checked for everything. They ended up saying that it was psychological."

"Like a little death."

"Exactly. The last time it happened I really thought I'd died. A friend of mine suggested that I get away. That's how I ended up here."

He looked at me curiously. "How long were you married?" he asked.

"Nine years."

"No shit. The longest I ever stayed with anyone was two weeks. Kids?"

"We always said we'd have kids. That was the next step, but it never happened. I mean, we always said that, but never tried."

"Affairs? Did you have affairs?"

I shook my head.

He looked at me closely. "It's like you're starting at year zero or something."

I smiled. "Yeah, something like that."

"Cool," he said. He seemed to be getting more and more interested in my case. "This is a very good place to be starting at zero. Everyone will be nice to you."

"Because I'm a foreigner?"

"Because you're a certain kind of foreigner. My advice is to try things. Try everything." He looked at his watch. "I really have to go now."

I walked him to the door.

"But wait," I said. "About the gigolo. When you say it alleviates desire, what do you mean?"

"Desire, I mean the emotional part of desire." He thought for a second. "You still function as an animal, but you're not in that horrible state of yearning."

After he left, I sat thinking for a while. For starters, I couldn't believe that I'd just met someone who was studying to be a doctor and working as a gigolo at the same time. Then I thought about what he'd said about "that horrible state of yearning." "Horrible state of yearning"—what was he talking about? Finally I remembered what he'd said about me. "My advice is to try things. Try everything." The thought of it interested me and gave me the jitters.

three

I received an e-mail from a girl named Leonarda that said: "I read ur sign. Plese I kneed to study English." I wrote back proposing that we meet the following day in a café with a red-and-gold motif near my place. I had never been inside, but had passed it numerous times.

I arrived a bit early and sat down. After a few minutes a man came over and asked if he could sit with me. I said I was waiting for someone. He laughed and began to sit down anyway as if he didn't understand. I shook my head more vigorously. It seemed he wanted something. I looked around. At the other tables were women sitting alone. Now I saw it, the situation, the way the women were dressed, in tight black, white and red clothes, with makeup on and very high sandals. I watched them wonderingly for a moment. Another man seemed to be approaching. Just at that moment, I felt someone grab my hand. It was a young woman with dark hair in a ponytail and startling green eyes under thick-rimmed glasses. She wore a baseball hat.

"This is a place for sluts," she said. "C'mon."

"It is?" Doubly surprised and confused, I gathered my things and followed her.

"Wow, you're really lost, aren't you?" she said, once we were out on the street.

"It did feel weird," I said.

"Those guys just want to fuck you in your butt."

"What?"

"Of course. Or haven't you read Naipaul's theory about the supposed Argentine propensity to brutal heterosexual sodomy? Turn around." She made me turn around and looked at my butt. "And you even have a nice butt. Which makes it worse—or better. I don't. Mine falls off like a little shelf. And you're foreign. And Ramplingesque!" She started laughing a lot. "The compliant victim. It's perfect. I guess you've seen *The Night Porter*?"

"Hey, wait a second," I was completely lost. "You're Leonarda, right?"

"Yeah. You can call me Leo, if you want."

"Why are you speaking English?" By now we were walking along Córdoba Avenue.

"Oh, I speak English. Who doesn't? I just wanted to meet you. I'm always interested in foreigners and I saw you putting up your sign."

"Why didn't you just say hi?"

"I was shy. Besides, you probably would have thought I was weird and been scared off. I do scare off people. And this way I could have time to tell if I liked you." She rolled her eyes. "Only now, well, I see that it doesn't matter if I like you or not. You need me. You're lost." Though she feigned exasperation, she seemed delighted by this news.

"Your English is very good," I said.

"Yeah, I'd only ever speak another language perfectly. I'm ashamed of Argentines who don't."

"You should hear me speak Spanish."

"Well, happily I don't have to." She shrugged. "Anyway, what I meant is that we Argentines always have to prove ourselves. We feel that we're so far away from everything, in the provinces of the provinces. No one even knows we're here. I'm like that too." She took a little skip forward. "I love my country. Hey, I know. Why don't we go to this meeting? I was going to go anyway until I got your message. C'mon."

I followed her as she hailed the next bus.

"What's the meeting?" I asked, once we were on the bus.

"It's this group called Mercury. They've created an alternative society, with their own currency and everything. Maybe it would interest you."

The bus was crowded. We stood pressed against the other people, hanging on to rubber straps.

"So what are you doing here?" Leonarda asked.

"I have a grant to study the waterworks of Buenos Aires," I said.

"Oh, wow, exciting," she said, in the most bored voice in the world. "Well, at least it's not the Dirty War or tango." She looked around, discontented.

"What do you mean?" I asked.

"Whatever. Those are the two things foreigners always study." Her face suddenly brightened. "Oh, but Sarmiento says one thing about water."

"Who's Sarmiento?"

"Just, like, the father of the nation." Her voice suddenly got rapturous. "He has a beautiful image, that the whole nation is a sickly anatomy. This Argie dude, Salessi, wrote about this. It was, like, right at the start of our history and Argentina is so big. Sarmiento said what we suffered from was extension, like this huge inert body of latent riches, but none of it moving around. Anyway, so what we needed to make it work was a circulatory system, vivifying fluids put in motion, interconnecting the different organs, giving life to the modern state. 'Because the greatness of the state is in the grassy pampa, in the tropical productions of the north and the great system of navigable rivers whose aorta is El Plata.'" She looked up, bedazzled.

"What you just said was a quote?" I asked.

Her face suddenly lost its rapturous look. She looked at me warily. "Yeah, why?"

"No, nothing, just surprised."

But her expression was strange. The change was unmistakable. Her face looked like it was disintegrating around the edges. I back-pedaled as vigorously as I could. "But I liked what you were saying. Please go on."

She looked out the window, then back at me.

"Are you patronizing me?"

"No, God."

She looked out the window again. "You swear you want to hear?"

"Yeah, of course."

"Okay." She took a breath and went on. "So it was like he was really talking about the waterworks of the whole nation."

I nodded, encouragingly.

"Oh, and the other part was about immigration. He said that, along with the rivers and railroads, immigration would be a kind of oxygen, promoting internal circulation and commerce. They were really try-ing to get people to come here at the time to fill that empty land. But not just anyone, that's the funny part. Sarmiento was very clear about the kind of immigration he wanted, Anglo-Saxon blondies like you because, he said, the instinct of navigation wasn't bestowed on the Spanish or Italians, but is possessed to a high degree by the people of the north. They would bring the spirit necessary to 'agitate these arteries.' And then guess what happened? Only the southern darkies came! Like me. I'm Spanish Andalusian and, even worse, with Peruvian Indian mixed in." She looked up. "Oh, here we are."

We got off the bus in a neighborhood I'd never been to and walked down a wide, straight street. It had rained the night before, the concrete in the shady spots was still drying. We came to a large gray-green metal door and Leonarda rang the bell.

There was no response whatsoever.

I felt a little nervous. "So what are we doing again?" I asked.

"It's a group of people who gather to discuss things. As I said, it's supposed to be an alternative society. And everyone's supposed to offer something, a service of some kind, like computer classes, or a haircut or blow jobs or whatever. And people are also supposed to propose things, projects in which everyone participates."

"Blow jobs?"

"Yeah, yeah, one guy was doing that."

We heard footsteps. After a moment, a young woman with thick brown hair cut close around her face opened the door. She had a patterned skirt and funky sneakers on. Leonarda introduced her as Milagros.

Speaking of circulation, inside there was a feeling of cool air circulating. It was a high open space, with old printing machines sitting here and there.

"They're all upstairs," Milagros said.

We followed her. In the room upstairs, people were lounging around on couches, two shoddy armchairs, a mattress on the floor, in the midst of a discussion. On a low table in the center were a few bottles of basic red wine, some plastic cups and a bottle of Coke. There was a trash can full of papers.

Leonarda and I sat down squished together on one end of a couch.

A man in his late fifties, poised on the edge of a chair, with gray hair cut short, a black turtleneck, looking at any moment as if he might leap up, seemed to be leading the discussion. Another man, younger, slightly plump, in his mid-thirties, with a swath of dark hair falling in his eyes, sat beside him, prompting him with questions. Now and then other voices chimed in.

"At one point I got interested in a group of Trotskyites," the gray-haired man was saying. "They had this literature, this magazine, and when I asked to see it, they said, 'Why?' 'Why?!' I asked." People in the group laughed. "'Well, don't you want people to know what you're doing?' The answer was 'No,' precisely no, they didn't. They didn't think there was any point in trying to disseminate what they knew. The question is what do you do when you're living in an age of stupidity and in possession of a truth that no one wants to hear? From the Christians to the Trotskyites there has been this model of a secret society. The secret society gathers to encrypt the truths that other people aren't ready to hear. What you have to do is think, not transmit. People in another era will be ready to hear."

The young woman, Milagros, looked up with a shy, slightly mischievous smile. "Was that your intention in starting this group?"

The gray-haired man, Ernesto, laughed. "Well, if it turns out that way. No, no, not really. What I had in mind was a strategy of happiness," he said. "We're confronted today with an immense amount of uncertainty. The idea of this group was to construct networks, or containers if you will, to alleviate the anxiety of uncertainty."

Leonarda leaned in and whispered to me, "That guy's the founder."

I looked around. The crowd was in general substantially younger than the speaker. There was a pale woman with delicate features and hair dyed bright orange, a young slender man in a purple turtleneck.

"The pending question is how are we going to organize ourselves?" Ernesto said. "At one point, we proposed that this group be something like a permanent assembly. But nobody wanted to do it, nobody wanted to take charge."

A guy with protruding teeth spoke up. "It's a problem of representation. Argentines don't believe in any representative system. Our short history has shown us only the errors of democracy, not its benefits. We always vote for representatives who betray us. All representation for us is linked to evil. We know that sooner or later we're going to get fucked over."

"Yeah," the young man with the hair in his eyes said, "which leads to a whole other definition of democracy. While in the United States, the concept of democracy arises from the American dream and calls into play such things as self-improvement, each person has the capacity to become better, in Argentina there's no idea of improvement, you are what you are. What democracy means to an Argentine is that each person does what he or she wants."

"Like in this group?" a voice piped up.

People laughed.

"In this group, nobody does anything!" Ernesto said. "That's the problem. Look, right here, nobody takes out the trash."

"But I think that's also why this group works well. Buenos Aires is an individualistic city." Milagros once again spoke up. "It's skeptic and that's part of its energy. Mercury in this sense is using the energies of the people of this city. There's a strategy here, to have a place to meet, we don't know how long it's going to be here or who's going to administer it, but we have a place. The agreement has to do with that."

"But isn't there a lot of energy lost that way? One of the keys of Mercury is to go toward the minimal effort," Ernesto said.

The pale delicate woman with the bright orange hair spoke, tilting her head to the side. "We were talking about putting together a project W the other day, a kind of V.I.P. Mercury, for a limited number of people. The question was can we transform Mercury society? No, let's not waste time. Instead of transforming the old society, let's make a new one. Here, yes, the rules will be very clear, whoever doesn't participate in projects with others during a determined time will be systematically left outside and the next candidate invited to join."

"Yeah, okay, I agree with that plan," Leonarda suddenly burst out. She spoke harshly, blushing, looking at the floor. Her sudden shyness surprised me. "But the issue is also how we participate. There's something in democratic stupidity that fetishizes certain words, equality, horizontality, and everything else falls on the side of 'bad.' Mercury is a good scenario for demonstrating this, there's always a kind of Mercurial police making sure that everything that's done here is participative. What's lacking is a more complex kind of thinking about the relationship between the individual and the group. What's needed is that someone in some moment takes the reins and pulls the others along. That way something gets done, instead of discussing how to make a flyer for four years."

There was an eruption of voices.

Leonarda leaned in and whispered to me, "C'mon, let's get out of here." She stood up and, ducking, snuck through the crowd. I followed.

We made it outside. Dusk. Long trails of eucalyptus leaves littered the streets. A small street dog trotted past.

"Sometimes those people drive me nuts," Leonarda said.

"I thought it seemed interesting," I said.

"Oh, yeah, it can be interesting. But I agree with the guy Ernesto, that it doesn't work the way it should. People are lazy. I don't like that at all."

She put her bag down on the ground under a streetlamp and got out her makeup case. She pulled a feather boa out of her bag. "Here, try this on," she said. I put it around my neck. It was a golden brown color, fox.

"Oh, that looks great," Leonarda said. "And besides, you need it."

"Why?"

"You're such a reptile. Feel," she said, touching my hand. "Your hands are so cold."

I wondered how she knew that my hands were cold. "Then what are you?" I asked.

She shrugged, looking cute. "A warm, furry creature."

"Somehow I doubt that very much," I said.

She laughed. She fumbled around again in her bag, pulled out some cheap apple-green block heels and put them on instead of her sneakers. "Okay, now makeup."

I had a little makeup on, not much. "Here, let me do your eyes," she said. She put makeup, more makeup than I'd ever imagined wearing, on my eyes. Then she took off her baseball hat and made herself up. Already, without the baseball hat, she looked transformed. With the makeup, she gave herself a kind of cat eyes, then put on cherry-red lipstick.

Along the street, there was a dark wash over everything, gleaming. As night fell, the streetlights, sensitized to the dark, went on one by one. Leonarda took my arm. We whisked around a corner covered with graffiti. The street was deserted, dark. I had read somewhere about the use of pharmaceuticals that make mice behave as nonchalantly as if they were taking a stroll, with the gravest dangers nearby. Now I thought of that. But I was already distracted.

The cars screeched by. They halted in a lurch at the light. Leonarda coughed, a deep lung-cough. "I'm exhausted," she said. "Let's go get a drink. But first we have to cross the railroad tracks." Her voice was suddenly hoarse. "It's dangerous there. Let's take a cab."

She stopped a cab. "Hey, you crossing the tracks? Can we come with you? We don't want a cab. We just don't want to be raped. Okay, great, thanks a lot."

We got into the cab. The area around the railroad tracks was deserted and piled with gleaming garbage. Leonarda stared out the window. "It's awful you're seeing Buenos Aires this way. It's because of the crisis, you know. But soon everything will get lovelier and lovelier."

The cab stopped on the other side of the tracks. "Hey, thanks a lot," Leonarda said, as we scrambled out.

We walked a few blocks. On a street corner up ahead were plastic tables and chairs set out as if it were a beach scene. A red strip of carpet led the way inside. The bar inside was dark, with storefront windows looking out. There was a large Plexiglas case above the stairwell.

"Ohhhhhhh!" a guy yelled when he saw Leonarda. He was holding his pink arms high in the air. Downstairs were small square mattresses, another little bar, with a tall bird of paradise stuck in a jar. The light was rosy. It smelled strongly of *nardo,* that nearly sickening flower smell. Leonarda and I ordered drinks and fell onto the mattresses. The pink guy brought us flowers.

"Are you married?" he asked.

Leonarda smiled. She looked at me. "I don't know if she wants to marry me," she said.

The pink guy went away.

"Were you ever married?" Leonarda asked.

"Yeah," I said. "I'm divorced."

"Really?" She looked at me, getting up on all fours on the mattress. There was something breathless in her face, rapt, delighted.

I nodded. I felt drunk already, though I'd only taken a few sips of my drink. Maybe it was something else, I thought. I felt a glimpse of a new feeling, woozy, reckless.

"Oh, I want to get married too," Leonarda said.

"You do?" I asked. It wasn't the way I pictured her.

"Is it marvelous?" she asked.

I shrugged. "It had its marvelous moments."

She laughed. "No, no," she said, still breathlessly. "I wasn't really thinking of marriage. I was only joking. I'll never get married." Her eyes were shining.

"Oh, well, I didn't mean that," I said. I lay back on the cushions. I felt careless in the nicest way. It was partly the drink, but mostly the presence of this woman who, I sensed, was really actually wild, while I myself was not. "Maybe you should try it. It's a kind of adventure, like everything else."

"Okay, maybe I will get married," Leonarda said. "But if I do, it will have to be in a funny way."

Later, in the bathroom, there was a woman moving slowly in front of the sink, completely inside herself, eyes hooded, impenetrable flesh.

"She's on something serious," Leonarda said.

She did seem to be in some interior fleshy bliss that had nothing to do with the world around her. She scooped up water from the faucet and put it in her mouth. She let her eyes droop even farther. She had shimmery gray powder on her lids.

When Leonarda and I went back upstairs, I was surprised to see a man down on his knees inside the Plexiglas case above the stairwell. He had shorts and a tank top on and was mouthing the words to a song. I lingered, watching him. The bad glimmer of the lights made everything look weary and greenish.

We walked out onto the street and asked for single cigarettes in a kiosk.

"Did you see that dude at the kiosk? Sometimes when people look at me, it's as if their faces dissolve in corrosive acid," Leonarda said.

I looked at her. I hadn't noticed it. Her face without her glasses looked different, extremely pretty when animated, but it could also, as now, look very exposed.

We passed some policemen.

"I want that hat," Leonarda said. She turned back around. "Heyyyyy, hiiiiiiii!" she said to one policeman, wriggling her whole frame.

"Hello," he said, stiffly, smiling, folding his hands in front of him. He felt better a few seconds later when his friend came over.

"Can I try on your hat?" Leonarda asked. "Just for a second?"

She reached up for it. The policeman flinched back slightly, then let her have it. She put it on herself, looked at him, looked at me, posed and then suddenly took off and began to run.

"Hey, hey," the young policeman yelled. "Come back here."

I didn't know what to do. I balked, paused. I'd never run from a policeman before. I was caught between the two of them, him and Leonarda, on the sidewalk. Then I began to run too.

Leonarda turned a corner, out of sight. I looked behind me. The policeman was running now too. He and his friend had thought Leonarda would come back. Now she'd disappeared.

Shit, shit, I thought. I ran. I turned the corner too. Despite her block heels, Leonarda was far ahead, looking back, laughing. She motioned me to run faster. She had hailed a cab. She jumped inside. The cab backed up toward me. The door opened. I jumped in too. Leonarda slammed the door and we were gone.

The young policeman stopped on the street, dropped his arms. Leonarda put her hand out the window and waved, then, laughing, turned back and sniffed under her arms. She took a tall aerosol can out of her purse and sprayed herself, both armpits.

"You want some?" she asked, handing it to me.

"Okay," I said. I sprayed myself in both armpits too.

The taxi driver glanced over his shoulder, displeased.

"Okay, okay, it's over," Leonarda said to him, putting gloss on her lips and the can back into her purse.

Later, back at my apartment, I stared out the window. Water ran in a sheen down the wall. My heart was beating.

four

I ran into Gabriel in the front hallway of the building. He had his bike helmet in one hand and was heading out.

"Hey, how's it going?" he asked.

I was happy to have something to report and told him about meeting Leonarda.

"Wait, she's in that Mercury group?" He was leaning against the wall, listening. "I know who they are. What does she look like again?"

I described her.

"Yeah, I think I know who you mean. I don't know her, but I know who she is." He stood up straight again, preparing to go. "Okay, I approve," he said, smiling his demon smile. "Here's my number." He gave me his cell phone number. "Keep me posted on everything."

I hadn't done anything for this grant project yet. I decided to figure out what I was supposed to be talking about.

I began with some basic Internet research. Starting big, I typed in "South America" and "water." Here is what I learned: the next big crisis this planet is going to face is water scarcity. With its huge sea of underground water, known as the Guarani Aquifer, South America is one of our main suppliers. Located beneath the surface of Argentina, Brazil, Paraguay and Uruguay, the Guarani Aquifer, named after the Indian tribe, could supply fresh drinking water to the world for two hundred years.

Interesting. I'd had no idea.

Next I looked up "Río de la Plata," the funnel-shaped water body on which Buenos Aires sits. "Hopefully named the Silver River by Spanish explorers in search of treasures, it has also been known as the 'Sweet Sea,' since visitors, confused by its size, mistook it for a freshwater sea." For centuries, enormous civic efforts had been dedicated to staving off the Río de la Plata's devouring of the city. Pushed miles back, the river, practically motionless to the eye yet ceaselessly encroaching, would then regain that terrain. Finally, accepting defeat, Buenos Aires gave up its dream of being a port city in the traditional sense and turned its back on the water.

I read on a bit farther and then decided to go out for a walk, directing my steps down to the coast so as to take a look at the river myself.

It took me about an hour to get there. A highway ran right along the coastline, on one side of which was the national airport. Small planes came and went. Taxis lined up. A sidewalk bordered the river itself. I waited on the far side of the highway for a moment to cross. Finally, it came. I dashed over. The river was contained by a high wall with a balustrade. I leaned over the balustrade and looked down. The water was velvet brown, gray in spots, rippling slightly, apparently so shallow that it only reached chest-high for miles. Far across was the Uruguayan coast. A few fishermen leaned against the balustrade holding their lines. Cars shot by on the highway behind them. There was no beach situation, no seaside terrace. Although elevated properties such as the penthouses of Libertador Avenue were coveted for their river views, tiny strips of glinting brown in the distance, it seemed that actually approaching the water was a different matter. The only loitering spot in the vicinity was a restaurant perched out on a distant pier, notorious, I later learned, as the place where men brought their mistresses but never their wives.

Walking along the balustrade, I passed a fisherman pulling up a wriggling catch, brown and silver. The cars roared by. A plane started lowering fast at a diagonal. There was a patch of green on the other side and I decided to cross over. The highway forked. I had to wait on a concrete island, cars whizzing by me on all sides. Relieved when I finally reached the grass, I walked on, crossing a bridge and another road, only gradually understanding that I had entered the vast park known as the Bosques de Palermo.

People in a paddleboat passed under a decorative bridge. Others sat together in the grass, they sat on top of each other, just sensing how it felt to be together, doing nothing, touching, body against body. Still others were gathering up their things, picnics, blankets, and heading home. I came upon an asphalt circle and began walking around it. Bikes whizzed past, then several joggers. On the outside edge of the circle, a figure dressed in purple satin had her back turned, head dipped forward. She was tying something at her neck. I looked over my shoulder as I passed, trying to get a glimpse of her face or at least something more, the front of her. But all I could see was the back view, legs in high heels, what looked like a short purple kimono tied with a sash. I walked on, passing a family, parents and two kids. The sycamore leaves rustled. A car cruised by. The traffic light was just changing.

Farther on, another figure—now I saw that it was a transvestite—in high white boots and white leather emerged from the woods and stood on the outer edge of the circle. Above her, the sycamores were shedding their leaves, yellow, brown, some of them still green. I looked around me. The first cars were already cruising slowly. Elsewhere men walked among the joggers with a furtive look.

I turned the bend and the scene changed. Here the lake was visible, the water reaching just to the brim. Any movement made it spill over farther, the ducks dunking their heads, the paddleboats. The swan kept its whole head and neck submerged for a long time. The little black ducks had tufts of feathers on the tops of their heads, their babies even smaller. The shimmering water flooded the grass, all that remained visible were the upper tips of the little green blades.

The trees with the bulbous trunks had graffiti written on them: "Flor, I need for things to go on happening between us. Your astronaut." Bicycles went by, Rollerbladers, not many. There was a white statue across the water, two figures, one seizing and kissing the other. The smell of the eucalyptus rose up, its shaggy aspect, hanging leaves.

People running, walking, biking, going round and round. I walked with them. Around the next bend, the scene changed back again. The prostitutes on the outer circle, standing, strolling, each choosing a territory, stepping out in front of cars. The air edged with darkness. A transvestite stepped out in front of a car, breathtaking in the headlights, in turquoise shorts and a halter. Another was dressed simply, in a skirt and black shirt. She stood in heels, a bit slouched. She looked like someone I had gone to school with, someone I could easily know. A car pulled up near her. She leaned down to talk for a moment, then climbed in. The car pulled off slowly. Where would they go? Back in the woods under the eucalyptus trees? Would they step out or stay in the car? It got darker. The families and joggers on the inner circle thinned out. I should go too, I thought. But I wanted to walk one more time around. The darkness was falling rapidly. I shouldn't be doing this. But I'd already taken the bend. Now there wasn't a family or a jogger in sight. I walked hurriedly, furtive myself, until I rounded the next bend and could see the avenue again. Peeling off, I made my way to it, where I finally slowed my steps.

five

Olga called. She was back from New York. Following up on her concern about me, she said there was someone I had to meet. "An Austrian woman. I was showing an apartment to a friend of hers yesterday and she came along. I'm sure you two have a lot in common." She gave me a telephone number, which I called that evening. The voice that answered was remarkable, a female's mezzo-soprano, deep, with flourishes. The woman's name was Isolde. She invited me to a gathering of a group of foreign women she was attending the following day.

The meeting was held in a spacious upper-floor apartment overlooking Libertador Avenue, one of those living rooms that you could have mistaken for a hotel lobby, with its smooth couches, glass tabletops and ceiling-high curtains that you pulled closed by a string. When I arrived, there were already about thirty women there, mainly American and British, a few other accents thrown into the mix, a Hungarian woman, two Norwegians. Sodas and cookies were laid out. A woman at a separate table was selling native crafts. Women were milling around, eating cookies, chatting and looking at the crafts. The street was far below, the air up here silent. You could see in the distance beyond the edge of the city a slice of quivering brown water, the celebrated river view.

I had arrived a bit late and looked for Isolde, but couldn't immediately identify her. Shortly afterward, the meeting began. I took a seat along with everyone else.

An Indian woman, Jannat, was in charge. She stood in the front, had a monotone voice. "First of all," she said, pointing to the crafts table, "everyone has to go and look at Sofia's beautiful scarves. I arrived ten minutes ago and I already bought two. Okay, let's turn to the business of the day. Louanne has very generously compiled for all of us a list of recommended maids, with addresses and phone numbers and previous employers. I really think we should give her a round of applause. She put a lot of work into it." Applause. "Another matter was the question of bringing natives to these meetings. Some people have said they're not comfortable with that. Louise, do you want to say what you think?"

Louise stood up. She was American, wearing pleated khakis. "I think it really defeats the point," she said. "What we want is a place where we feel safe to say what we want without hurting anyone else's feelings. There's support here and understanding. We want to feel that we're not alone. Above all, we want to be able to complain. If there are Argentines in the room, we don't feel comfortable doing that. I think we should make a very firm policy. See your Argentine friends somewhere else."

Jannat looked out at the room. "Do people agree?"

A discussion ensued. Another woman, Mary, broke through. "I wanted to propose a subgroup among us. I'm married to an Argentine, as many of us are. I think this means that a lot of us have certain problems and concerns that it would be very helpful if we could get together and discuss. Like, I don't know, what it's like to be married to an Argentine!"

Laughs.

"I thought we could meet for dinner once a month," Mary said. "And pick American places, or at least American food, for a treat. Like T.G.I. Friday's."

Another woman stood up. "I'm Liv."

"We know you, Liv!" Liv, it turned out, was the group's Swedish chiropractor.

"Mary and I discussed this before and I think it's a great idea. The problems I have with Carlos aren't problems I can discuss with Argentine women. No matter what I say he acts like he's a Paraguayan refugee, and I'm the privileged one. But it's not true. It's the other way around. He grew up with maids. But why do I always act like he's right?"

"It's our politically correct guilt!" Mary said.

"That's right," Liv said. "That's what we decided. It's the Third World–First World dynamic."

"Hey, instead of feeling guilty, why don't we just say to them, 'Look who's on top here, look who's running the world'?" Mary suggested.

Laughs.

A Wednesday-night dinner was agreed upon for those married to or living with Argentines.

"I'd like to introduce myself," a very different voice said, deep and rippling, with an Austrian accent. I turned and looked behind me. It had to be Isolde. It was that same voice. I saw now that she was a woman whose look had been thought to perfection, smooth, blond, rich-looking, a kind of Belle du Jour, only she was sturdier. Her plumpness, the one glitch to her perfection, pointing to a fragility, made her somewhat touching. "I'm Isolde. I'm from Austria. I'm very happy to meet you all."

"Hi, Isolde!"

"I'm working on a project that I wanted to share with you. I think we all have a great opportunity here, to make links or—how would you say?—ties, between Argentina and the rest of the world, and I believe that one of the most effective ways to do it is through the arts." She seemed slightly nervous, which made her arresting voice vibrate even further. "A lot of Argentine artwork never leaves this country. What I would like to propose is a small foundation to make these links, connect these people. I have some connections in the Austrian art world. I'm sure you all have some too in your native countries. The big art fair here in the spring is a great occasion because what's interesting, of course, is the exchange, artists from abroad showing here and Argentine artists finding an audience abroad. Do any of you know Florencia Lacarra? No? Well, I recently went to a show of hers. Now she's a very talented Argentine artist. I'm sure she'd find representation in Austria, if only that link were made. The truth is I actually don't remember ever seeing an exhibition by an Argentine artist when I was in Austria, and I went to plenty of exhibitions. Now this is shameful. Wouldn't you agree?" There was silence and a few murmurs of surprised assent. Isolde, with her looks and accent, if not the content of her speech, was unmistakably making an impression.

I found her afterward at the snacks table and introduced myself.

"There you are," she said. "Helloooo."

We were quickly interrupted by several of the women who had been impressed with Isolde's speech. Flushed with her performance, Isolde was gracious and kind.

"But the truth is I can't imagine any of these women throwing soirées for artists from abroad," she said under her breath, pulling me aside. Even as she talked, I could tell that she was assessing my clothes, which had seemed fine when I'd left my apartment earlier but now, compared to hers, looked rumpled and mismatched. Her own look was the opposite, everything pressed, fresh, clean, with touches of both milkmaid and matron. "Don't you see? They could never give a glamorous cocktail party in their lives, never *really* glamorous. They wouldn't know what to wear, who to invite." We were standing by the floor-to-ceiling windows, looking out. "How I would die to have an apartment like this." She turned to me with her generous schoolgirl smile. "I'd give wonderful parties, wouldn't you?"

In the elevator downward, she was still in a buoyant mood. "We're going to get coffee, right? But first come with me for a second. I want to show you my new cards." Stepping outside, she led me to a copy shop down a side street. Her cards were ready. "See," she said. The card was cream-colored with italic script: "Concierge international artistique."

There's a pretty place with a garden right this way," Isolde said, leading me to the Museum of Decorative Arts. We sat down outside at small iron tables under the tipa trees.

"So how long have you been here?" I asked.

"Four months in this part of the world. My friend Sabina and I went to Uruguay for the summer season. Then, at the end of February, we came here. She went back after a few weeks. But I stayed on."

"And you like it here?"

"Oh, yes, there's wonderful culture." She leaned nearer, and spoke behind one hand. "And everything's so cheap. I actually have tickets to a concert at the opera house tonight. Do you want to come?"

"Oh, I . . . can't tonight," I said. I didn't have anything else to do, but that seemed like a long day to spend with someone I'd just met. "I'd love to another time.

"Have you met nice people?" I asked.

"Oh, yes, wonderful people." She gazed off distractedly.

But Isolde's show of reserve was only momentary. A few more questions and the whole of her story came tumbling out. Although I wasn't yet aware of it that afternoon, I was soon to find myself in the role of her primary confidante.

Isolde, thirty-five, was from a small Austrian village. The men in her family were veterinarians with modest but dependable veterinarian incomes. She had a sister. I imagined from what she told me that the girls were lovely, strong, on the side of being big-boned. They were sporty and always known to be among the prettiest in their classes at the village school.

It was the elder sister who from a golden girl turned one day into a dark figure. Her parents had had great plans for her—she was to be the first woman in the family to go to college—but then things didn't work out as they'd hoped. The sister botched her college entrance interviews. Her male admirers were soon turned away by her aggressive habits. It was said that she had a mental disease. She stayed at home, locked in her room, only coming out at mealtimes to tyrannize the family. She had a child with a man, who then ran off. She brought the child to live with her in the house, another golden girl, but whose life was shadowed from the start by her troubled mother with whom she shared a room.

Isolde was apparently a simpler character, lovely but not so lovely as her sister, without such a feeling of entitlement, the good-natured one, innocent, hopeful, someone to whom life happened, one thing led to the next, with minimal forethought on her part. She was in a sense the face of the family. Though utterly inexperienced, she would step out and represent them in the world. This was, at least, how her parents seemed to feel, now that their dream daughter had failed them. Obediently, Isolde took on this role, going to college in Salzburg, studying commerce, getting a job in a bank. None of these things did she do particularly well, even by her own estimation, but she did them. In college, she fell in with a different sort of crowd, people with more money. She already had this glamour girl look, which, more instinctively than through calculation, she began to cultivate, copying other girls' clothes and hairstyles, mannerisms and accents. She spent a lot of time on the clothes question, looking at magazines, browsing through stores. A natural gift plus a great deal of dedicated time soon meant that she surpassed the other girls, more born to that world, with a tasteful, glamorous style that all of them envied. Then too, working in a bank and having her own money kept her steadfast in this path.

The one surprising thing she'd done was to suddenly one day quit her job at the bank.

Her parents were dismayed but, for the first time in her life, Isolde didn't care. She had saved some money and set out to travel. Her first stop, as she'd told me, had been Uruguay, a destination for a certain category of Europeans at that time of year, the southern summer, and then Argentina a month or so later where, seduced by the reception she received, she stayed on. "It's different, isn't it?" she said. "The way you're treated here is different." She laughed. "Like royalty or something." In Austria, she'd been nothing particular, an Austrian among Austrians, blonde among blondes. She'd even dyed her hair darker in school in the hopes of distinguishing herself. But here she felt revered. Why? Simply for being European, already she was placed in a higher echelon.

Her first encounters in Argentina were lucky ones, or so she thought at the time. The initial connection was made through her landlady to a guy, now in his fifties, whom the woman's daughter used to date. The guy had a right-wing TV talk show, one of the most popular in the country. Isolde didn't entirely grasp the heavily right-wing connotations of his commentary, nor would she have particularly cared, but the guy was famous. He invited her to barbecues at his country house. She was let in on the secret of that crowd. The famous right-wing talk-show host, always seen publicly in the company of a famous actress, and not least known for his misogynist jokes, was actually gay. He had a young beautiful lover the age of his own son. The two boys lived in his house, shared meals with him, each had a room with a DVD player and powerful speakers. Isolde felt one of the elect to be privy to this secret. She tried to relish in her rapid, unpredictable insider status. But the truth was that, when she was among these people, in this walled-in property outside the city, eating the famous Argentine barbecue, nothing touched her soul. She soon realized that it was a false piste. Where she wanted to be was with the cocktail crowd.

She backtracked, refused some of the country invitations. Though she'd started a flirt with the talk-show host's son, she dropped this too. There was a whole cocktail circuit. Isolde spent many lonely nights, knowing there was a cocktail party somewhere and not having anyone to go with or not being sure that she could get in. Sometimes she got dressed up and went anyway. She could almost always get in with her face and clothes alone. All the same, she would feel terribly exposed as she stepped out of the cab and up to the door. When no cocktail event was materializing, she went to modern dance performances or concerts. Everything, as she'd mentioned, was so cheap.

She soon met a French girl her age who was secretive and would sometimes tell her where an event was and sometimes not. The French girl had her own agenda, to be the most sought-after foreigner in Buenos Aires. Though the French card among Argentines could never really fail—the model for the upper-class Argentine woman is French, for the Argentine man, British—Isolde, with her goldenness, was competition.

In the cocktail set, circulating is key. On the other hand, given this very fact, the eloquence of absence cannot be overlooked. Isolde was not so good with the eloquence of absence. She had no patience with being alone. She was savvy enough to know it should be tried. She would try it and couldn't bear it, would dress hastily and go out. The French girl, Isolde's nemesis, was much more savvy. She could abstain. Evening upon evening would go by and she wouldn't appear. The thirst for her would grow, more and more eyes trained on the door. Isolde would see the longing eyes. She noticed these things. She'd vow to herself next time to abstain, but the next time would come around and she would be there.

Moreover, Isolde was healthily lusty. Within the upper-class circuit was a skein of brothers and cousins. While at the college she'd gone to, sleeping with one or another person was considered quite normal, she had no idea how small this world was. One night, after plenty of champagne, she slept with a guy after a party. Immediately, the word got out. It was actually the other brother she'd been interested in, Lucio, but now he backed away. Or rather, he still let her approach him, but now had a little smirk on his face whenever her name was discussed. She soon understood that she had tarnished herself. She'd lived in Austria and London, had traveled throughout Europe. Yet it didn't matter. She was in this small circle now. It was like an insect trap, sticky. You put your foot somewhere and the move was irremediable. It was stuck there for all to see. Still, no matter what, the Austrian card was strong.

Isolde imagined herself working as cultural attaché, in the embassies, hosting parties. Or in charge of a charity group for children. The funds would be raised at cocktail parties. Most appealing was this idea of being ambassador to the European art world, all the more so as her conception of it remained so vague. Only later would I learn what her actual situation was that, running low on money and without a job, Isolde had taken to asking discreetly at cocktail parties if anyone knew of any work she could do, to the delight of a certain bevy of snickering Argentines.

Walking home afterward, I thought about Isolde, cutting her path here, as I was cutting mine. I remembered what I'd learned at the botanist's about invasive plants. Once in a foreign environment, some species simply shrivel and die. There's too much moisture or too little. The seed can't get a grip in the ground. Others, however, due to the lack of the delicate balance of natural controls, suddenly grow rampant or metamorphose, a calyx, for example, hypertrophying. The foreign air, the soil, touches something in them. A part of their character, maybe dormant before, is suddenly pricked to life.

six

The e-mail I'd been waiting for from Leonarda arrived. "Hey, I'm on lab duty today. Searching for the virtual equivalent of the Ebola virus. You wanna come by and pick me up @ five?" She left an address. I didn't have the slightest idea what she was talking about, but I was definitely going.

It was in a neighborhood I'd never been to, Boedo. The streets looked disheveled. The eucalyptus were in a state of constant dishevelment, tumbling down, falling over themselves. Imported trees, they weren't even from here originally. The smell, depending on atmospheric conditions in your head, could be bracing, soothing, intoxicating. I tore off a bunch of leaves, crushed and smelled them as I walked.

Following the street numbers, I soon located a white door. There were three buzzers. How to know? I pressed the second one down, then the third right after that. But before anyone had time to respond, the door opened and a lithe young man slipped out, letting me enter behind him.

The yard inside was muddy with sprouts of grass. Wooden boards had been laid out to step on. On the far side was a low structure like a garage but longer, with a wall of windowpanes. I followed the wooden boards to the structure's door, which was ajar.

A short hallway led to the main room. The room gave an impression of glass. Besides the windows, glass shards were piled up against the wall. Something big had broken. Everywhere people crouched over computers, some old, some new, a few with their backs open. A printer had been taken apart. There were cords everywhere.

At first I didn't see Leonarda. Then I did. She too was crouched low over a computer, with her baseball hat and glasses on, fully concentrated.

Only when I got very near did she look up. "Hey, you came!" she said.

"Yeah," I said, as if there might have been some question. I looked around. "What's going on?"

"It's that group, Mercury. They do experiments. Everyone's given a task. Or you can propose things. I proposed taking the Ebola virus and making it virtual. It's been something I've wanted to try for a while. Here, this is Facundo. He's developing a new form of digital animation."

Facundo, thin with a shaved head and standing as he worked, gave me a nod.

"Why don't you take a look around? I'll finish up and we can go."

I walked around. I passed the fine-featured woman with the orange hair who had been at the other meeting. She had a large set of earphones on and was listening with concentration, her eyes half closed. A small, round girl with a short fringe of bangs was peering at a monitor. Beside her were several iguanas in a glass cage with electrodes on their heads.

"What's that girl doing with the iguanas?" I asked Leonarda as we were walking back across the muddy yard.

"She's monitoring their sleep. Seems they only sleep with half their brains."

"Why's that?"

"Sleep's dangerous, dude. They're protecting themselves."

"Hey, isn't the Ebola virus lethal?"

"Duh," she answered.

On the street again, Leonarda stopped and put down her bag. "Okay," she said. She took off her hat and T-shirt—underneath she was wearing a black-and-green negligee—and got out her makeup case. "Here we are, back in Planet Gorgeous."

I'm bringing you to a place where you can meet a ton of guys, okay?" Leonarda said. "Isn't that what you want? To meet guys?"

I laughed. "Maybe," I said. I hadn't thought about it.

"C'mon." She put her arm through mine and pulled me along.

The bar was in the center of town, Libertad Street. We went up a set of stairs and turned to the left and, indeed, the place was packed with men. The aesthetic was modern, glossy black tables, glass vases here and there containing single flowers on long stems. A silver bar stretched the length of the room. Courageous single women sat alone at the bar. The men milled around. They were in their thirties, forties, some looked older, a few preppy guys looked even younger. They were, on the whole, all dressed well and well-groomed.

Due to the no-smoking law recently passed in the city, the bar had constructed a little outdoor patio, a glass box, where you could still smoke. The box was dense with smoke. Here and there, you caught the shape of a head or limb pressed against the glass.

"Let's sit at the bar," Leonarda said.

"Are you sure?" I asked. I looked around. "But won't people bother us?"

"Well, ye-ah. That's the whole point. Guys will talk to us."

I looked around again, thoroughly daunted by the prospect. It had been ten years since I'd been in this situation.

"C'mon," she said, already sitting down.

We ordered cocktails, Leonarda, a strawberry daiquiri, a mojito for me.

"So how are you finding us aborigines?" she asked. She made the sign of a monkey, pretending to scratch an armpit with one hand. I'd noticed before that her armpits were shaved except for one dark tuft in the center.

I smiled. "Surprisingly advanced."

"We're so grateful to you for bringing us your wisdom. Listen, can you do me one favor? Don't get all romantic about the crash, okay? Foreigners come here and they make a big deal. Then there are, like, these super-romantic newspaper articles in the foreign press about countries that otherwise never get discussed, like describing the apocalypse or whatever. When the point is this shit happens to us all the time. We're used to it. Every eight years, there's a crash. In eight years, there'll be another crash. Big fucking deal."

"Okay," I said. It was true that I'd been having some romantic thoughts in this respect.

She looked at me differently. "Have you ever been close friends with a girl?" she asked.

"Yeah. Haven't you?"

She shook her head, her face in this moment very exposed. She was smiling, but then her tears came quickly and suddenly. "Oh, no, I don't like how I'm being," she said, wiping them away brutally with the back of her hand. "I want to be different with you."

"That's okay," I said, patting her back.

"Don't treat me like a dog."

I hesitated for a second, then said, "Good little dog," and went on patting.

It turned out to be the right calculation. She laughed and in that moment, we were interrupted by exactly what we'd come for, guys. Since we'd arrived, they hadn't taken their eyes off Leonarda. She'd removed her glasses and was showing considerable cleavage with her negligee.

"Where are you girls from?" a man with a red sweater over his shoulders asked.

Leonarda quickly perked up. "Estonia. I am, and she's from Latvia."

"Really? Hey"—he turned to his friend—"these girls are from Estonia, and what was the other one?"

"Latvia," I said.

His friend, blonder, leaned in too.

"Do you like Buenos Aires?"

"We love it," Leonarda said. "We're neurologists. We've come to study the effect of Viagra on jet lag."

The first guy made a swirling motion with his head, indicating confusion. "What?"

"Yeah, we carry Viagra with us all the time," Leonarda said. "We have some on us now. We love it. It's great for women too."

She turned to me.

"See," she said, softly, "isn't this fun? Now the really funny thing would be if we kissed."

"Really?" I asked.

"Yeah, then they really don't know what to do."

"Okay," I said. If I had been wearing glasses, I would have taken them off.

Her mouth seemed bright and full of teeth. She was laughing. "Are you ready?"

I nodded. If only I was drunker, but we'd barely taken two sips. It seemed she was always doing this to me, acting crazy before we'd even had time to get drunk. Unlike me, she clearly didn't need to drink to behave in any way she pleased.

She put her hand on my back and brought her face near mine. She kissed me very gently, almost too gently, lightly, it was like a butterfly, with just a little bit of tongue.

The gesture did cause a stir. Before, there had been a little space around us. Suddenly, there was none. Was it an illusion? It was like something I'd seen in an Antonioni film, Monica Vitti standing on a ledge with white stone stairs below. More and more men gather on the stairs, looking up at her, hemming her in. The place now seemed to be wall-to-wall guys, with leering male faces everywhere we turned.

"Oh, shit," Leonarda said. "Let's get out of here."

She slipped her arm through mine and pulled me off my stool. She was crouching down, slinking, moving through the crowd.

"Hey, wait." I lumbered behind, realizing we hadn't paid. I hadn't picked up on this habit of hers of going places and leaving without paying.

As we headed toward the exit, the crowd pressed even tighter. Was it my imagination? Suddenly, they were frantic, pawing and pulling at us. One guy's arm went around my neck from behind. I lunged my head back and shook him off.

We rushed down the stairs. A few of the drunker, younger guys were following. We made it to the street. Leonarda took my hand and we ran. Several guys came tumbling out the doorway, yelling. One or two began to run after us, then stopped.

We turned the corner of a street and were in a plaza, lugubrious, half lit, with those huge, squat, sprawling trees, the ombu, their trunks and roots undulating like human bodies. There were people on benches making out. Oh, I remembered, we just kissed. I looked over at Leonarda shyly.

But she was already on to something else.

"C'mon, I want to show you something," she said.

She stopped a bus and we got on. Because of the crowd, we were separated slightly. I was glad for the distance, which allowed me to be alone for a moment and absorb what I was feeling. It seemed to me that everything was quivering, the lights, the sidewalk, the leaves on the trees and the dark, huddled shapes of people walking by.

"Here we are," Leonarda said after a while, reaching over some-one and pulling on my sleeve. We both stepped down from the bus.

I felt something touch the back of my hand, Leonarda's hand. We were going through glass doors and then were in an elevator. The elevator was shiny with mirrors. On the fifth floor, we got out, Leo-narda leading the way. I followed her down a series of nondescript halls, turning once, then again and again and again. How could she remember the way?

Next thing I knew we had stepped outside. We were in a garden, but it wasn't just a garden. It was a whole landscape, a rooftop park. There were palm trees, a lawn, flower bushes, a swimming pool. Insects and birds flitted around.

Leonarda led me by the hand past the swimming pool to the far edge of the rooftop, which looked out over the neighboring sky-scrapers. In the far distance we could see the rippling brown water of the Río de la Plata.

"All this used to be underwater," Leonarda said. "One day it all will be again."

She dropped my hand and ran toward the flower bushes. They were a variety of jasmine. She picked some, smelled them. I fol-lowed. We lay down on the grass. The sky turned pinker, bluer. A blot of cloud passed. I was looking at the palm trees, wondering how deep the dirt was, how the roots held. The blades of grass curved downward. They were long enough to curve, and green, so green. Were they actually even real? I sat up. Was any of this real? It was misplaced, of course, an entire ecosystem transplanted to this unnatural height. Suddenly I saw it in eerie colors, the artificial green of a mint drink, the chemically treated turquoise swimming pool. I lay back down.

"Listen," Leonarda said, "I've been thinking. If you want to do this with me, I think it would be great. Together we could make the perfect being."

seven

If I felt with Leonarda in the presence of a highly developed mind, about thirty times more active than my own, the synapses firing all at once, with Isolde, it was different, even the contrary. She seemed to know what she wanted, wealth, glamour, upper-class status, all swimming in a concoction of cocktail parties and art. At the same time, there was something unconscious about her behavior, even brute-like. She pressed forward, without seeming to understand herself in the slightest. She went after things, would butt her head against them again and again, then wander around dazed. When she was desperate, you had the same impression that she was an animal, dazed, reeling around in front of you. On the other hand, she seemed very alone and her bravado touched me. She made me think of heroines of novels I'd read, Lily Bart, Madame Bovary, a Lily with Emma's aspirations. Going out to cocktail parties and putting on airs without a cent to her name.

Isolde and I met for lunch, we met for tea. She would call to tell me the news—the French girl had caught Ignacio, the most eligible bachelor in BA. Or she'd call in desperation, urgently solic-iting my advice about one or another of the trials in her life. Bub-bly, affectionate, she would sometimes call three times in a row. One guy, a Brazilian diplomat, with whom she was flirting while simultaneously badgering him for a job, put it this way—"Your phone behavior is perfect for finding work, but disastrous if you're looking for love."

After one of our meetings, she had arranged to see her landlady. "Oh, please come with me. I can't face her alone today."

I agreed. Besides wanting to respond to her plea, I'd been told about this woman and was curious.

Isolde's entire existence in Buenos Aires was predicated on her living arrangement. Isolde's aunt had been the lady companion to a wealthy old Frenchwoman. It was through this Frenchwoman, a fourth cousin to Isolde's landlady, Beatriz, that the connection had been made. The unspoken requirement in exchange for an apartment where Isolde needn't pay rent were these weekly visits. Isolde would sit by the bedside while Beatriz talked.

The apartment was in Barrio Norte, spacious—Beatriz had had five children—but now the only illuminated areas were the woman's bedroom, the kitchen—the domain of Clara, the Paraguayan maid—and the pathway between them. The rest of the rooms lay in darkness. Once Clara had let us in, we followed this pathway straight to Beatriz's bedroom. The bedroom was like a little girl's, with frilly things everywhere. Beatriz lay in her bed with a white mask of makeup on and glittering eyes. A mirror, makeup and creams were on the side table. Each morning, Isolde had told me, she put on a dense layer of makeup and in the evening she took it off.

Isolde introduced me. "Hello, dear," Beatriz said, staring at me hard for a moment. Then she turned away.

Isolde had told me that she suspected Beatriz of judging her and disapproving. On the other hand, it seemed clear that Beatriz was also trying to impress.

Clara came in with a tray of tea. She was dressed in a pale blue maid's outfit. "In 1910, in the Campaign of the Desert, led by General Rojas, the Indians were all wiped out," Beatriz said once she'd left. "That's why you don't see Indian traits among us. Shortness, dark skin, flattened features. In other South American countries, you will see those things. But we Argentines are European. You can find all my ancestors in the Recoleta graveyard." She batted her eyes slightly. "It's ridiculous, but people here think of me as Lady Di."

During the daytime, Beatriz lay in bed and watched TV. She collected horror stories from the news. This was her main subject, Isolde said, since the crisis. She relished in repeating the stories she'd heard, about people getting their purses ripped out of their hands by motorcyclists or being held for ransom in their houses, mistreated, fingers cut off.

"No one's safe anymore," Beatriz said now. "Never go out alone. The city's not safe. It's a terrible thing to live alone. Don't you see? Everyone's moving to gated communities. Clara? Call Clara. Get her to call you girls a cab."

I dropped Isolde off at her apartment, let the cab go and began to walk. Isolde's loneliness had been palpable that day. Should I have lingered on with her? I pictured her in her apartment, a smaller version of the woman's apartment. Although the arrangement was that she could stay as long as she never brought anyone back there, she had once shown it to me. I pictured her retreating to the bedroom, which she'd told me was the only place she felt comfortable.

It was still early, 2:00 P.M. in the afternoon. Familiar with my own loneliness, I had no trouble imagining Isolde's. The day stretched before her. What should she do? She'd glance at the cultural pages of the newspaper, where she had marked certain events. If only she had, at least, an evening activity. A cocktail party was preferable. She'd heard there was one at the Portuguese embassy. Though she hadn't received an invitation. Usually it didn't matter. Still, in her mind, there was always the doubt. And then there were the agonizing moments, inevitable if you went to these events alone, when you floated there, waiting, with no one to talk to, pretending to be utterly riveted by the art. No, she wouldn't go. She wasn't feeling strong today. But what, then? She couldn't bear either to stay at home, all afternoon and then all night as well. A movie? A modern dance performance on her own?

The foreigner's loneliness should not be underestimated. Anyone who has felt it knows what it is. At first, Isolde would sense something like a dark liquid dripping into her chest. She'd grow more and more uneasy. She'd get up, try to do something, shake herself, dress or change her clothes. But even here, while dressing, usually for her such a pleasure, the beautification of her already very pleasing frame, nothing correction, all enhancement, the level of the dark liquid would be rising. As she put on her pink lip color, picking up the glow in her pinkened cheeks, she'd already feel the futility. Why? What would it matter? She felt herself isolated, cut off, behind glass.

She'd make up an errand, talk it up to herself, "Yes, this'll be good, this is what I've been meaning to do," step out, start the errand. But already by then, the city seemed blurry, as if she couldn't see it. Everything was grayed over. She felt herself stumbling along through this gray landscape. Making it to the shop where the errand was to be performed was a feat in itself. She was incredibly tired. Then she had to go inside, confront someone. She wouldn't just leave, no, she cared too much for appearances. But along with the darkness came confusion. She couldn't even entirely remember what the errand had been, what exactly she'd wanted, a border around the collar of this dress, but was it really this dress? And she, who had normally such a good eye, doubted if she'd ever be able to choose the right border in this moment. After a brief, muddled conversation with the seamstress, she postponed the errand and left the shop.

Now what? The streets were truly gray, washed over with gray. She didn't want to go back home. She sat down in a café on the corner. The loneliness overwhelmed her. Now it appeared as a dark pit in front of her. She was falling, falling in. She tried to claw her way out, frantically, like an animal. People moved around inside the café. They passed by on the street. No one knew, no one knew anything. She was clawing at the sides of a dark hole. There was nothing she could do. But she had to do something.

She would call someone, that's what she would do, anyone. In her cell phone she had a list of contacts, assiduously collected at social gatherings. She called a girl who was somewhat of a friend, though she didn't trust her, Australian, Melody, a complete butterfly. Melody wasn't there. She left a message. Then she called Melody several more times in case she actually was there. She called me. I also didn't pick up this time. Next she started calling one by one down her list of contacts, putting on her best voice and upper-class accent, richly melodic in the extreme, "Hello, it's Isolde. I just wondered what my great friend was doing tonight, I'm free." Sometimes she'd call twice, or several more times for good measure, throwing away all her manners, ruining, in many cases, all her chances, with this man or that very sought-after society hostess, toppling the delicately assembled social edifice she'd been constructing so carefully over these months. But at least, momentarily, the calling brought relief. The illusion of contact, if not contact itself, soothed her enough, so that she could safely stand up and, braving the pit, leave the café and make her way home.

eight

When I was working for the botanist, he lent me a book one day about the Cambrian Explosion, that pivotal biological point in the history of life on earth when an astounding diversity of animal life, nearly all the species we know now, appeared in the course of a relatively short time. What provoked it? Theories abound. Geochemical perturbations, unprecedented cell structure mutations, a dramatic lift in oxygen levels, allowing animals to radiate spectacularly. But no one explanation has proved conclusive. Those first months in Buenos Aires were something like my own little Cambrian Explosion. In the same way, not just one event, but a combination of converging factors in my life, some interior, some exterior, provoked this situation, some which I can identify, others which remain less clear. Later I would wonder—how important was geography? Would it have happened elsewhere? Would it have happened were I not in that paradoxically fertile posture, on the brink of despair? Whatever the causes, the effect was clear. Buenos Aires, dead, came alive to me. But it was not only that. Through Buenos Aires, I was able to see the universe in a way I had never seen it before.

Gabriel was an important presence. And Leonarda was, of course, a defining factor. It was in her presence that Buenos Aires first came alive, but then as with certain drug experiences that you can reproduce later without taking the drug, the city would stay alive for me or rather, simply, it became a world I could see. So, I began to wonder, what had I been seeing before? A partial view, episodic, not only large parts of the world, but large parts of my brain—is not the brain the world?—in darkness. Suddenly, I became obsessed with spreading as much light on my brain as possible. I had an image that kept recurring of unraveling all the wrinkles in my brain and laying it out in some fertile field.

June came. Winter. The light changed. Everyone was shivering exaggeratedly, but the truth is it wasn't that cold. I'd still go out walking. I walked a lot. Sometimes Gabriel stopped by, before or after a client meeting. I continued my water research, visiting the Palace of Waters, once the storage deposit of Buenos Aires drinking water, now a museum devoted to the water question. I met up with Isolde, over coffee, drinks, or joined her when she had tickets to a cultural event. But at the center of my life were my outings with Leonarda. We'd get dressed up and go to parties. We'd go out dancing. Or we'd go to bars and talk to people, mainly men, lying about everything, who we were, where we were from, forcing them to follow a train of logic that then doubled back on itself. We confounded them, it was all make-believe, and then just as we reached our apotheosis, some final absurdist conclusion, we were out on the street again.

Suddenly, thanks to lying, I detached myself from my biography.

Rather than ruminating over things, I forgot about my past. Of course. Who has time? Leonarda had no interest in her past either.

"Childhood," she would say with disgust, "who wants to talk about childhood?" Rarely, it seemed, did a memory cross her mind.

What she did like were ideas. She was enamored with ideas, above all, her own. Nostrils flared, she would walk along spouting them left and right.

At other times, she was full of mistrust. I could see her face turn. I'd done something, said something that made her suspicious. "Look, there's not actually a problem here," I'd say. "I swear. I'm not asking you to trust me, but trust me at least on that one small point. There's not a problem here. We were having a nice conversation. I liked what you were saying."

Sometimes I could soothe her, sometimes not. When I couldn't, her eyes went depthless, animal eyes. She was only out to save herself. I learned that the best thing to do in these situations was distract her, tease her, if at all possible, make her laugh.

One day, she took a picture of me, in which, by some trick of the camera, I looked like a monster. She seemed afraid. She quickly made an excuse and said she had to go.

A day or two later, I received an e-mail, "Heyyyyyy, hiiiiiiiiiiii, you have no idea how much you want to see me."

I felt deeply moved. When I wasn't with her, I felt concerned about her, imagining her in the clutches of her horrible family.

For my part, I was learning how to play. These nocturnal adventures, slinking along walls, lanes, gardens, chasing someone, being chased ourselves. There was playfulness in every tendon and digit of her form. Unless she got moody. Then she walked along, shoulders hunched up, eyes fixed on the ground.

There was her childish thievery. I soon understood that she was doing it for me, as an offering of sorts, which both confused and enraptured me.

She aspired to sophistication, glamour, not so much wealth itself, or that wasn't the focus, but knowledge of things such as jewels, wine. She aspired to beautiful manners, which she practiced well enough, if a bit ostentatiously, until she forgot, something caught her attention. She hulked around, grabbing at things. This even when she was dressed in a miniskirt, with a tiny tank top only half covering her large boobs. One thing for sure was that she was ambivalent about her beauty, would dispose of it in a second. A part of it too was that there were so many different things she aspired to.

She was twenty-eight and lived with her parents, I never saw where. I gathered from her stories it was a little apartment and maybe she was ashamed. Certainly her clothes were cheap, though at the same time suited her so well.

I also gathered there had been some political activity in her family's past. Her mother had been involved with an urban guerrilla group. This she told me proudly one day. "They're monsters," she said another day, her face twisting in an ugly way. "No, they don't interest me at all."

She was engaged in a militaristic campaign of her own, on the one hand purely aesthetic—she liked military clothing—and on the other, intellectual. She demanded that the Left account for themselves, investigate their own actions during Argentina's Dirty War. Enough of the victim role, if they ever want to be taken seriously. It was a provocative stance, and promised to get her into all kinds of trouble, which, it seems, was precisely what she wanted.

Without understanding what was happening, I felt youth reviving through my limbs. The opposite of Gombrowicz, I would look in the mirror and find myself young. Night after night passed— how do I explain these nights? I see black squares, one after the other falling. I would be with her. We'd go parading about, or I'd be alone, lying on the floor of my apartment. The building was silent. I'd feel the blood in my veins. Did anyone know I was here? It didn't matter. I felt hidden here, sensing without understanding this strange revivification.

Sometimes I would stop to wonder what my old friends would think of Leonarda. And my parents? Occasionally, I'd feel shocked by things she said. But this intrigued me too. Part of the attraction was what I thought of as her different morality.

She took me places in the city I would never have gone to. Once, we passed by a nightclub called Solid Silver. "It's a sex show," Leonarda said. "Have you seen one? C'mon." The show wasn't on. The guy standing at the door didn't want to let us in. Leonarda suddenly changed her physiognomy entirely, standing very near and pressing her face into the guy's face. "Listen, buddy, we're journalists. We write for *Time Out New York*. We're reviewing the place. You're lucky if you show us."

It seemed to be the last thing the guy expected of her. He looked over his shoulder.

"All right, you can take a look."

We went down the stairs. Below was a bar and a stage with colored lights. The floor was carpeted. There were several poles around which women were practicing their routines. Some of them were dressed in sexy outfits, others in sweatpants. The only spectators were a couple, an old man and woman, sitting side by side on square stools and watching.

"Wow, that's great," Leonarda said, looking at the couple. "But I don't know about the girls. I think we should come back and see them in their splendor."

Within a second, we were on the street again. It was always like that. Leonarda lived under the sign of speed. Everything with her developed so rapidly, went by in a flash.

But the door to youth was a strange one. It opened into a dark vestibule. What made it youth for me was that it implied action. In my actual youth, I had been in a melancholic posture, overly receptive, the membrane between myself and the world very thin. Now, with her, I was learning a new strategy.

She told me on one of our first "dates" that she thought she could actually learn something from me, which she didn't feel about many people. Arrogant, of course, she had plenty to learn, but I took this as a compliment. "I used to hate this city," she said to me one day, "but when I walk through it with you, everything seems glorious." Another time, she said, "I've never loved anyone before." She was speaking with urgency, gripping her small, hot hand in a fist. "I don't know how to do it. You're teaching me."

Initially, I brought some reasonableness to the proceedings. That is, until she touched something in me and I would be set off, act wild. I would want us to lie down in the grass in a tricky neighborhood late at night. Then she would be the one to be reasonable, calm me down, pull me up. I gave her that gift—she could play that role with me.

We went to the port for a drink. The walls of the hotel bar were lined with antelope heads decked with pendants and pearls. In the dining room alongside, there were rows of white unicorns with red eyes. Outside was a perpetually overflowing swimming pool. We ordered the house cocktail.

"I used to work for these guys writing texts in English," Leonarda said. "The owner of this place is, like, an ex-model. He always wears white suits and snakeskin boots. Most of the other investors are Russian. They're doing a whole renovation of the port. It used to be totally seedy down here. The truth is the whole thing was a mess from the beginning."

"What do you mean?"

"The water's too shallow. They used to have to leave the big boats really far out and bring the stuff in in little boats pulled by mules, totally inefficient. Then they invited this engineer guy Bateman over from England—I mean, really, why couldn't these guys think for themselves?—but the yellow fever epidemic hit and he chickened out. Those morons. Well, at least they finally decided to make it look half decent."

I looked at her. "You have a lot of information in your head."

She rolled her eyes. "Yeah, you poorly instructed foreigners are always so impressed with us Argentines knowing a thing or two."

We sipped our drinks.

"Sometimes I feel like you're colonizing my brain," I said.

She looked at me. "What do you mean?"

"I don't know," I said. "It's as if you're trying to control me, in some sort of post-colonial gesture of revenge. And you're doing a good job."

She laughed. "I guess you're not as dumb as you look."

Later we were walking back to the city. Between the two places, the polished renovated port and the city, was another of those uncertain zones, deserted, maybe a remnant of the seedy port—the pavement was crumbling, grass grew up in tufts. Through it ran a gleaming set of train tracks.

As we were nearing, a cargo train passed, just a few wagons, carrying what looked like coal. Or was it just bricks and rubble? It stopped, then was going very slowly. A young man looked out. All we could see was his dark face. He saw us.

"Hey," he yelled softly. "Hey, girls, come along."

We looked at each other, stalled. Should we go? We began to run toward him. I was ahead, nearing the train wagon. I almost leaped. "Wait," Leonarda called. I stopped.

Part II

nine

Argentine Lucio Mansilla wrote about his days in Paris in 1851: "The Marquise, who was 'charming' and who undoubtedly found me appetizing, well, I was very pretty at the age of eighteen, invited me to dinner and organized a party to show me off. When the meal was over, there was a reception and after the introductions I heard 'the beautiful ladies' saying: 'How handsome he must look with his feathers.' Of course in hearing this compliment, I preened, 'je posais,' an expression that doesn't translate well, but at the same time I said inside myself, 'What beasts these French are!'"

The foreigners in Buenos Aires invite the upper-tier Argentines to theme parties, tea parties or Thursday-night wine parties. These are foreigners with money. They have tasteful apartments, on Arroyo, in Recoleta. The Argentines go, playing their role, as upper-tier Argentines, Third World aristocrats. They pose, they're amusing, and utterly amenable, mixing with the foreigners, speaking different languages. Unless you were watching closely and were suspicious—and most foreigners aren't—you would never catch the glances shot between them. But already, among the Argentines, in the paneled elevator downward, the mockery begins.

While the foreigner, much as he wants to be liked, also feels somewhere deep inside that he's really done the Argentines a favor, by being here in this country at all, and then associating with them, inviting them to his home, the Argentine is overly conscious of the foreigner's absurdity. Feeling, despite himself and solely for the amorphous quality of being foreign, that the foreigner is superior, he at the same time finds the foreigner vulgar, ignorant, poorly instructed, even lacking physical harmony. The woman's head is too big. The German has the rabbit features of the inbred. A few satiric comments exchanged, the Argentines walk away down the evening street with their beauty intact, this natural beauty that springs up effortlessly, mysteriously, generation after generation, according to a correct application of the laws of reproduction.

Isolde had invited me to accompany her to the German's Thursday-night wine party on Arroyo Street.

When we arrived, the room was gradually filling. The floors were laid with small amber-colored pieces of wood, the bookshelves the same color. The German, Thomas, was in his early thirties. His neck jutted out. He had a slight stutter and a post in an overseas German bank. "Welcome," he would say to whoever appeared, too formally, too eagerly really to be gracious. Despite the regularity of these events, he continued to be flabbergasted at the very idea that a woman, much less a strange woman, would step into his home.

As we walked around, Isolde told me who was who. Tatiana, the beautiful upper-class drunkard, whose father was a famous artist, had recently returned from abroad. She had a look of discontent on her face. A small band of women, who had been in the nerdy group at the best girls' school in Buenos Aires, were now, as then, still ostracized at these parties, even if they had made names for themselves elsewhere in the world. One, Bettina, was a well-known clothes designer. Yet this made no difference. In these settings, she was still, as always, an outsider, pressed into a corner. So why did she still come?

Ignacio arrived. In him was encapsulated the whole point of this class, its good looks, easy charm, privilege taken for granted. His brothers and cousins were versions of himself, each with aspects, but in no one else had the elements been so fortunately combined. Ambitious women roved around him. He was the only one the French girl had agreed to date. Though he kept his apparent cool, he was actually terrified by these women, including the French girl and, as I would witness later, would eventually end up settling with a very different type of girl who asked nothing of him, never complained.

"What's going on with your art world project?" I asked Isolde as we milled around.

"Oh, there's interest," she said. "Plenty of it, at least on the Argentine side."

With Argentines, there's the constant urge to get the word out, abroad, we are here, we exist. This corresponds to a real set of circumstances. Unlike in the States—where an internal career can largely suffice—it is one thing to have a career within Argentine borders and quite another to have one abroad. The foreigner is consequently stamped with this glowing and vertiginous possibility: though the foreigner might him- or herself have no contacts whatsoever, have grown up in the Midwest, in a little town, he is conceived as rubbing shoulders with luminaries, in the New York art world, the London jet set, immediately preconfigured as a messenger to the court, by virtue of his foreignness, as if like the first conquerors, he and he alone were bringing back news to the King and Queen. Some foreigners, you can see it in their faces, are simply baffled to be placed in such a position and miss entirely the role being handed them. Others, more astute, play their cards. Isolde knew how to play her cards. What was less clear was what she actually meant to do with them, once played.

Later, Leonarda appeared. We'd spoken earlier and I knew she might be coming by. "Heyyyyy, hiiiiiiiiiii!"

I'd told Isolde and Leonarda about each other, but they hadn't met.

Isolde was talking to our German host. Her blue-and-white dress gave an impression of crispness, cleanliness, while her flat gold sandals matched her jewelry. Now I watched Leonarda watching her, always on the lookout for what a foreigner could yield.

"More colonial material?" I suggested.

"Maybe," Leonarda said. As always, when she was interested in someone, I felt jealousy mixed with curiosity about what she would do. "You see," Leonarda whispered to me, "the way she's totally adopted the upper-class accent?"

I nodded, though the truth was I hadn't understood where Isolde's accent was coming from.

Leonarda leaned into Isolde's conversation. "Your Spanish is delightful," she said.

"Oh, yes, I insist on speaking Spanish," Isolde answered. As usual, while smiling, she scrutinized people's clothes. Leonarda wore a tiny wool skirt and a piece of lacy lingerie as a shirt.

"When did you arrive?" Leonarda asked.

"A few months ago."

"Like Daisy. Are you having fun?"

"Of course," Isolde said. "There's wonderful culture here." This seemed to be her line. What was less predictable was its effect on Leonarda.

"Really?" Leonarda's eyes were shining. It seemed that, despite her cynicism, she was very susceptible to foreigners admiring her country. "What have you been seeing?"

"Opera, dance. There's wonderful dance."

"Oh, you're Isolde! Did you see *Tristan and Iseult*? It was just playing at the Colón."

"Of course. Did you go?"

"No, I couldn't." Leonarda looked horribly disappointed, then enraptured again. "But I have the music. I've been singing it." She sang a line from an aria, really quite loudly. "But *you* should sing. Your voice is amazing. You must be a mezzo. Have people told you that?" I could see her dreaming up the scene, Isolde, internationally celebrated mezzo-soprano, quivering in the footlights. These infatuations of hers always made me nervous.

"I have been told that, yes."

"And are you going to stay here? You must stay. We can study singing together," Leonarda went on, as if nothing else had ever mattered to her in the world.

Isolde laughed, touched and surprised. I, on the other hand, felt annoyed. For one thing, I couldn't sing.

"What else have you been doing?" Leonarda asked.

Misinterpreting the question as "What do you do?" Isolde adopted her upright posture, forceful, as if exerting her will. Were it not such a sensitive issue for her, Isolde would have undoubtedly understood by now that most Argentines would never pose a question like that, considering it bad manners, and would be perfectly content to learn weeks later, for example, that a newfound friend was responsible for assuring the security systems of the U.S. government or worked in a Turkish restaurant as a cook.

"I'm developing a project related to art and charity for children," Isolde said.

"Sounds fantastic," Leonarda answered, her enthusiasm taking an abrupt nosedive. Neither "charity" nor "children" were at all her thing.

"Good, good," Isolde said, relieved not to have to elaborate.

In the end, things never worked out between Leonarda and Isolde. The three of us attempted to meet a few times, but something always went wrong. For starters, Leonarda was always afraid that people would find her weird.

"She's sort of weird, right?" Isolde asked me right away.

I shrugged, as befitted my role as the cipher, the malleable, mediating one.

Unsurprisingly, in Leonarda's case, it was more complicated. She would go into raptures, dreaming up her image of Isolde, the innocent Austrian woman in distress. "She's adorable, her accent. She's so alone. I can picture her so well wearing a dirndl." But when face-to-face with Isolde, something always jarred. Isolde did not cooperate with the dream. She kept getting in the way, asserting her will. "No, let's meet at this restaurant instead." "Let's only speak in Spanish." "I'm not going to be ordered around by some poorly instructed Austrian" was Leonarda's conclusion.

On seeing Leonarda at the party, a slim man with dirty-blond hair got down on one knee.

Isolde, on my right, appeared agitated. "Do you know that guy, Alfonso?" she whispered in my ear.

"No," I said. "Do you?"

She put her hand on my arm, a bit flushed. "Here," she said. "Can we talk over here?"

"Sure."

We moved backward toward the bookshelves. "I've made out with him a few times at parties, always drunk, of course," Isolde said, her eyes half on me, half on Alfonso. "And then he asked me on a date. I knew about his family. You know, he's from a very old Argentine family." It seemed that Isolde had memorized this whole new set of nomenclature, so different from the European one. "He plays the role of the upper-class eccentric. But what I hadn't realized was that the family was poor."

"They are?"

"Can you believe it?"

"How did you find out?"

"Because I got all wet. There was a big storm and the car window wouldn't close. Alfonso got out one of those tools, what is it, a screwdriver. He told me to put it in the door handle and turn, while he went around outside, getting soaked of course, and pulled the window up with his hands. But it wasn't a new thing. The window had been broken like that for years." She looked up and gazed at Alfonso again, still mooning over him. "He never called again. Someone told me that Alfonso only likes dark-skinned women, so maybe that's what happened, I don't know."

Leonarda rejoined us, as a shaggy-haired man sauntered in the front door.

He wore a long dark green leather coat and a thin scarf around his neck. It was an interesting concoction, cool dude mixed with dandy.

"Oh, gross," Leonarda said. "Look who it is. Hi, pig."

The guy turned. "You're looking rather monkey-ish yourself," he said. He pointed to the tufts of hair under Leonarda's arms.

Leonarda turned to us. "This is Diego, a horrible guy I used to date."

Diego snickered. "I don't think 'date' is the word. That sounds pretty harmless. What you did was much worse."

Leonarda scowled. "Given the material, I think I was kind."

"I don't believe you," Isolde said to Diego in her luscious voice. "What did she do?"

Diego made a hex sign. "You don't want to know."

"No, really, I don't believe you. She seems divine."

"Maybe so. Maybe that's the explanation. Divine wrath."

A little while later, as I was coming in from the balcony, I happened to catch a scene. Isolde was standing with a small contingent by the front door. Several guests were leaving. The standard greeting in Argentina, both hello and goodbye, is the one-cheek kiss and you're pretty much required to give it to everyone in the room. Bettina, the designer, had done her rounds. Diego, who had only stayed briefly, was just finishing his. He arrived at Isolde and, instead of turning his cheek sideways, aimed for her lips and stuffed his tongue into her mouth.

ten

"That Mercury stuff's going nowhere," Leonarda said. "It's all talk, but they don't *do* anything. Like I presented them with this whole project to do cultural terrorism, but nothing came of it."

"What's cultural terrorism?"

"Whatever. I'll tell you later. Listen, I've decided we have to go it alone. I think it's time we embarked on the Master Plan."

We had just passed the prison on Las Heras Avenue, now turned into a park. The prison had been of the panoptic variety—I'd seen photographs—a central point, with wings radiating outward, architecture as vigilance strategy, the idea being that from that central point, you could see what everyone was doing at any given moment anywhere on the premises. Now there were patches of green, flowering trees. The purple jacaranda blossoms dropped down, translucent trumpets. The pink palo borracho ones were star-shaped, slightly rubbery.

"What's the Master Plan?" I asked.

"You'll see."

She was carrying a stick of *nardo* in one hand and an ice cream cone in the other. She smiled. "You're a very important part of it," she said.

"I am?"

"Yes," she said. "So is someone else, the prey. See that building?"
Up ahead on the corner was a building in gray stone, with a semi-circular entranceway on pillars. "It's called The Palace of Pigeons.
This was one of the few buildings historically where it was okay to
retire into aristocratic poverty. The prey lives there."

"Another aristocrat?"

"No. Just a snob. He's a famous writer. But he's more than that.
He was, like, a member of a leftist group in the seventies, a TV per-sonality in the nineties. He's done everything. He's our Argentine
Renaissance man."

"And why's he the prey?"

"Because I have a plan."

We stopped at a light. "To seduce him?" I had to admit I didn't
like the idea.

She shrugged. "If necessary. I want to control his mind."

Due to her changeable aspect, Leonarda possessed entrance to
all kinds of scenes, the upper-class and foreigners circles, the
underground art world, university student parties. Often, in the course
of an evening, we'd pass from one circle to the next—Leonarda was
particularly skilled at the quick exit. Shortly after this conversation,
Leonarda and I made our first foray into the literary crowd. The prey
was winning the National Argentine Prize for Literature.

Leonarda came by my apartment to pick me up. Knowing that
we were going to a bookish event, I had dressed bookishly. She

looked critically at what I was wearing. "No, no," she said, "we have to look fabulous."

"I feel like my butt is very prominent in this dress," I said as we got out of the cab on Parana Street.

"That's good," Leonarda said. "Because your butt is also part of the Master Plan."

On her side, she was perfectly naked under her corduroy coat, which stopped just above the knee. Or at least that's what it looked like. Not a stitch of other fabric was showing.

I followed her through a wrought iron doorway. The place was a converted mansion. Inside was a plaque on the wall that said "Built in 1913 by the Allemand family." We entered a passage lit with low yellow light, what had formerly been a garage.

"The hunt is on," Leonarda said.

I tried to suppress a giggle. I had never done anything like this before.

She looked over her shoulder, then back. "I don't want to wound him right away. This is just about letting him know that I'm out there, that I'm after him. I want him to start getting scared.

"Oh, wait, lipstick," she said. She got out a mirror and a lipstick tube and began reapplying a deep red. She had already explained to me that lipstick was meant to represent blood on the mouth of women, making them attractive.

"Why would that make them attractive?" I had asked.

"It goes back to primal times, when a red mouth showed you were lucky and healthy, having just devoured prey."

Was this hunting metaphor actually getting us anywhere? I wondered, as I applied more lipstick too. Yet in another part of my brain, I heard drumbeats. I pictured us strapping on weapons. We resumed walking. We were two against one, but she didn't see it that way.

"I don't need you here," she said. "I want you here. I can handle the guy perfectly well on my own."

We reached the far side of the yellow passage and stepped out into a garden. Ivy covered the walls. There was a bathtub to one side full of water, with goldfish flitting around inside. Champagne was being served on a table along the wall. A white stone staircase led upward from the garden to the second floor. Leonarda stood, a bit slouched in her high heels, checking out the scene. She suddenly changed her posture and moved into action. This was the point where her social fears, her pathological shyness, collided with her ambition. The shock could yield some interesting results. "Come on," she said, "let's check who's here."

We got glasses of champagne and climbed the staircase so we could look down from the terrace above. She pointed out heads, trashy history writer, novelist, filmmaker, right-wing journalist, backs of heads, tops of heads, a face just turning, dark, gray, curly.

"Okay, I'm bored," Leonarda said. She turned around. The house rose up behind us. "Come on, let's look inside."

From the terrace we stepped into several large, open rooms, where the Allemand family used to entertain. There was a DJ set up beside the piano, a service area to one side. Above on the wall was a projection of a large rose-like flower, pink, white, red, circling slowly.

A set of steep stairs led to the next floor. It was darker here, quiet. This was where the family had had their private rooms, slept, dressed. We went through a door, then crept down a hall past a bathroom. We heard giggling voices. A couple in a corner room was smoking a joint. We passed through. In the adjacent room we stopped. A dark window looked down on the garden, a whole other view. We were high up here. Vines bounced in the wind.

"We have to go back down there," Leonarda said, as if it were a condemnation.

"Do we?" I asked. "Why?"

I felt it too, dread.

She looked at me. She didn't have her glasses on. She had her exposed look, then didn't.

"Because we have to," she said. "The plan dictates that we have to. Come." She took my hand in her little hot one. We went back downstairs. "Let's smoke," she said.

We asked a woman at one of the tables inside for a cigarette and stepped out on the terrace to smoke.

Down below was a cluster of people posing for a photo op. "That's the artistic literary establishment, though they'd never call themselves that," Leonarda said. "In their minds, they're still the avant-garde. He belongs there too."

"Where is he?"

"He's not there. He must be preening for his prize."

There was an announcement at the back of the garden, a woman at a microphone.

"This is a show event, you realize. The prize is all rigged," Leonarda said.

We were watching from above. The bald head appeared, glint-ing. "There he is," Leonarda said. She seemed to rise up like some animal. The guy stepped out, receiving the prize. But it was like on a battlefield, you couldn't see anything, a blur of movement, a body part in the way, then just in front of you a head looming, it ducked, you had a squinted view into the distance, but then there were people moving one way in a herd, stopping, turning, forced the other way.

Though we couldn't see him, we could hear his voice now. The prize, he received it, was accepting. His voice was remarkable, as everyone knew. He'd done radio, television, politics, literature. "He's done everything, everything," Leonarda said. "That's the whole point of him."

And then it was over, dispersion, milling.

"We need to meet him." She was thinking. I could see it, I had faith in it, entirely, the rapid firing of her brain. "He's going to go off somewhere now with his friends. We have to find ourselves where he is." She spotted a cluster of people down below. "We have to step into the inner circle," she said.

"The inner circle?"

"I'm sure they've reserved one of those upstairs rooms."

I felt that our lives had gotten suddenly complicated, after that glorious position of floating above.

"We do?" I asked.

"Yes, we do." She seemed nervous, even full of trepidation, but also eager.

We were approaching the inner circle, we'd already greeted some of them in passing. Now we were getting nearer, plucking fresh glasses of champagne on the way, standing, installing ourselves.

"Are you naked under that coat?" a woman asked Leonarda.

"She's important, the Madame of the social group," Leonarda whispered afterward to me. "That's her husband, a filmmaker," she said, nodding toward the handsome, younger man standing just left of the Madame's shadow.

Oh, but soon, he'd arrive, the monster. Soon we'd all be gathered here, the monster in our midst.

I turned to look and, lo and behold, there he was, tall, chest puffed out, the shiny head. He had some scars on his face. His language was absurdly eloquent, his eyes sad. He had just won the prize, the biggest prize for literature in the country. He was probably more puffed up than usual.

Where were we going, now that he was here?

We were with them, following them up the stairs. We made it to the upstairs room, on the corner, overlooking the garden. It was small, crowded now with all of us inside. There were red plush couches and chairs.

Yes—the inner circle all looked at each other—finally we're alone.

Leonarda and I were being tolerated as anomalies. But, faced with the challenge, not of the group but of this man, Leonarda was in her prime.

We sat down for drinks at a table.

I was talking to the handsome husband. On her side, Leonarda was directing herself to the others, and most precisely to the prizewinner. He was sitting, his long thin legs out of sight under the table, his body puffed out. Leonarda faced him, talking.

Then she was saying it—it was her line—others listening. "The Left has behaved so cowardly. When are they going to examine their own actions? It's disgusting, it's degrading, the way they take on the victim role. We're all waiting, my whole generation is waiting, for some act of recognition, that would represent true valor. We want heroes we can believe in, not these sniveling wretches. Oh—" She paused and covered her mouth with her hand, looking at him. She giggled. "Well, anyway, that's what I believe."

There was silence. No one spoke. The prizewinning leftist looked at her bedazzled. He was the one to answer, who was supposed to know the answer, the war hero, yet he was speechless before her. She knew it. Never had she been so powerful. It was in her face, eyes, the tilt of her head, the way she held her shoulders, her whole delicate frame. Then the moment passed. He rose, puffed up again, laughed at her.

Still the door had been opened, the moment occurred. She turned to me. Triumph, her green eyes fiercely glowed green. Looking back at her, I too felt it, a mixture of exhilaration and the chills.

eleven

"Okay, tell me more," Gabriel said. We were in my apartment. He had had a long night and was lying back on the chaise lounge. I had been telling him about the Master Plan.

"Do you know this guy?" I asked, referring to the famous writer.

"Of course I know him. Everyone knows him. There's no way *not* to know him." He seemed amused, indulgent, if a bit wary. "So the plan is to hunt him down?"

"Yeah. Can you believe it? I've never done anything like this before," I said.

"Me neither," he said. "I'm wondering how it works. And what the end result's supposed to be?"

"We catch him, I guess." I laughed. "I don't really know. You're the one who said I should try everything."

"You're right, I did." He thought for a second. His face, tired like this, had its mournful look. "This Leonarda sounds very compelling."

I flushed. "She is."

He hesitated, looking down, then up again. "I guess my only point would be to make sure you're trying things for yourself, not other people."

I was surprised at how little he seemed to understand. "But I am, don't you see? All this is entirely new to me."

He backed off. "Yeah, yeah, I understand. I'm not saying not to do anything. My only advice would be to keep your mind free."

His wariness seemed weird, especially coming from the apostle of freedom. But, I decided, it was probably just his mood.

W e're preparing to send a second installment of funds at the end of the month. Please let us know how you're progressing." Shit. The grant people. It was September. I'd been here for six months. The agreement was that they'd send me the second installment of funds halfway through, once they'd received a brief progress report. If they didn't send the money, I was in trouble. But I also hadn't done any research for a while. I decided to check out the Riachuelo, the river, notoriously contaminated, that marks the line between Buenos Aires and the suburbs in the south.

I looked at a map and got on a bus that seemed like it would take me to the Barracas neighborhood, bordered on one side by the river. The bus wound on and on through the city on what seemed to be an incongruous path. Apart from a slight feeling of wooziness, I didn't mind once I got a seat by the window. I had brought some reading with me about the river and the areas around it. I looked at it as we rode along.

This neighborhood, in the southern part of the city, had once been home to the wealthy, I read, until the yellow fever epidemic chased them north. The servants, largely black, stayed behind and were wiped out, another reason, along with the black troops sent off to fight the Paraguayan War, that the black population in Argentina, once sizable, had been so decimated.

As for the pollution of the Riachuelo, it seemed that it was hardly new news. As far back as the 1870s, the British engineer Bateman, hired to tackle the port problem, expressed horror at its filthiness and even cited it as an obstacle to the reconstruction of the port. The resultant "city of Bateman" plan traced a blueprint for the modern city of Buenos Aires with its storm drain and sewer systems and—this part was new to me—underground streams. In the 1940s, the construction of a web of subterranean rivers began. There was a striking photo in a brochure I had picked up from the Palace of Waters of men at the end of an underground tunnel leaning on their shovels. I looked up, gazed out the window, then down again at the map of subterranean waterways, many under streets I walked every day, oblivious of the secret water city underneath.

Had I missed my stop? I went to ask the driver, who told me it was the next one, a bus terminal, the end of the line. The river wasn't immediately in sight. I started walking one way, felt I was definitely off track and turned the other way. There was a chain-link fence, a jacaranda tree. Then I saw it, a glimpse. I was coming up on a bridge, small, cement, with sidewalks on either side for pedestrians. I stepped onto the bridge and walked out to the middle. The water below was moving slowly, almost curling, like molasses. On the banks were mudflats. Trash littered the flats. The smell was not so bad here or the wind was just right, I wasn't getting it. Out of the corner of my eye, I saw something floating, near the right shore, a russet-colored shape, familiar. Then I understood, it was a dog's back, most likely an entire dog, its legs hanging down out of sight.

I looked across the bridge. I knew the city ended here. The Ria-chuelo was the limit. In the distance, on the other side, I saw people walking on the streets, some carrying bags, out shopping. There was smoke rising, a smell of something burning. I decided to go across. I crossed and began walking up the street. I passed a supermarket, stores. I stopped in front of a hairdresser's and looked in the window, then stepped inside.

I'd never had an elaborate beauty regimen, but would regularly get a haircut and have my eyebrows plucked. I'd noticed that morning that my eyebrows needed work. In the States, my hairdresser had plucked my eyebrows too. But this time, when I asked about eyebrows, I was sent to the back, the waxing area. A woman in her late forties, with short dark hair and a round face, greeted me, introducing herself as Vera.

"What do you want to do?" she asked.

"Eyebrows," I said.

She patted a high vinyl bed with a large sheet of paper over it. "Lie down here," she said. In one corner were metal bowls of hot wax and a spatula.

She had an accent. "Where are you from?" I asked.

"Belarus. You?"

"The States. The U.S."

Her Spanish was good, if quirky, as was mine, only our variety of quirkiness was different. Still, we managed to communicate pretty well.

"Are you married?" she asked.

Wow, I thought, cut to the chase. "No," I said. "Are you?"

She smiled. "Second time."

"Happily?" I asked.

Vera shrugged. "I say to him—'One day I'll just go down to Retiro and get on a bus, whatever bus, and see where it takes me.'"

I felt a bit jittery in a nice way. Only in a beauty parlor could you arrive at this place in a conversation so fast.

"What happened with your first husband?" I asked.

"He died in Belarus. Gangrene. You know what that is? When the blood stops flowing. It happens a lot in cold countries. The arteries get blocked. Nothing's circulating and the limbs just die. He had to have one amputation after the next. First they cut off his big toe, then the next toe."

"Jesus."

"The doctor said smoking made it worse. He had to stop smoking. But Dima couldn't stop. The doctor said, 'Stop smoking for your wife.' He couldn't do it."

She had waxed my eyebrows and was now touching them up with tweezers.

"Dima never used to drink, which was rare for a Belarusian. That was actually what I had liked about him. I'd been in love with a different guy from my high school. We had been going out together for four years. But when he came back from military service, he was drunk all the time. He worked in an auto factory. I'd see him around on the streets. He'd be totally drunk. It was a small city. I hated that."

She dabbed a little cream on the skin around my eyebrows and passed me a hand mirror so I could inspect them. She had shaped the arches very nicely.

"Great," I said.

"Anything else?"

I hadn't been planning to do anything else, but I also wasn't ready to leave. "Like what could I do?" I asked.

She laughed. "Everything. Armpits, legs, toes, down here." She pointed between her legs.

"Okay, I'll do legs," I said.

I had never done this before. We both waited for a second.

"You have to take off your pants," Vera said, seemingly delighted by my awkwardness.

"Oh, yeah, right." I stood up and took off my blue jeans and lay back down again.

Vera went to stir the wax.

"How did you meet your husband?" I asked.

She came over and put a strip of hot wax on my leg.

"He worked in the company where I did. I was twenty. It was a marketing studio. We sold stuff to shopping malls. One day, he asked me to go out for coffee. The next day he came to work with his document and asked me to marry him. I went to meet his family. Neither of us had gone to university. But the people in his family had. His mother was a professor, his father a lawyer. They played chess. I fell in love with them.

"When there's a lot of love, there's a lot of suffering," she went on.

She tapped on the strip of wax on my leg to see if it was dry, then pulled it.

"Owwww!" It hurt like hell. I looked up at Vera. What the hell was I doing to myself?

"Oops, okay, it's always the worst the first time. You have to breathe in." She pressed my shoulder back down on the bed. "I'll tell you when." She put another strip of wax down.

"But Dima and I weren't in love, we respected each other a lot. He was a wonderful companion. We had fights sometimes, but it didn't matter. We were always doing things. We'd stay up all night talking until six in the morning, then have coffee. Or we'd play cards. I always lost. Okay, breathe."

I breathed in. She pulled the strip. It still hurt, but not quite so much.

"We had a little quinta, where we went to work on the weekends. We'd bring the kids. We went fishing. Or collected herbs or nuts, which we dried on the roof and sold at the pharmacy. You could get a certificate that said you had sold herbs at the pharmacy, which meant you could buy an imported piece of clothing or shoes. Everyone had money, that wasn't the problem, there just wasn't anything to buy. Okay, breathe."

"Things started to change when he got the gangrene. They had to cut off a foot and then a leg. He started drinking and got aggressive. He felt a lot of pain. When he was drunk, he didn't feel it. He didn't want to be an invalid. We found out he could get a prosthesis in Germany, though it cost a lot. There was a war vet, from World War Two, who had one. He said to us, 'Your husband's still young, he can do it.' But then they cut off the other leg. Breathe. By now, he was staying in the clinic. We would visit him. He was jealous and thought I had a lover. I didn't have a lover. I didn't even have time to think. Okay, turn over."

I had been lying faceup and now lay facedown. She put wax all over the back of my legs.

"Finally, it was his birthday. He went to a friend's and got so drunk that the ambulance came. He died three days later. His organism was too weak to sustain all that alcohol."

"My God," I said.

"I cried a lot. I cried all the time during those years. That's why I never get depressed. I've never been depressed because I always cry. Okay, breathe."

I thought about how hard it was for me to cry. Maybe the inverse was true for me. I'd been depressed for years because I hadn't cried. But before I could get to the end of that thought, Vera ripped off another strip. Another searing pain, that left my whole body quivering.

She returned to the pot of wax. I lay there thinking for a second. "What did you use to do in Belarus?" I asked.

"I was the manager of a hotel."

Vera's situation in this sense was exactly the opposite of Isolde's. Argentina for Isolde had meant instant promotion. She had leaped ranks for essential reasons, she was Austrian. Vera had stepped down, joining the ranks of that worldwide league of immigrants who live in states of demotion, whose present occupations reflect in no way their past ones or the ones for which they've been trained. She had arrived eight years ago at the age of forty, with her children in tow. Coming here was a way for her son to avoid military service, which she wanted him to do, as it could be brutal. Through Belarusian contacts of her brother, she had gotten a job as a prep cook in a kitchen. She went each day to help the cook, chopping vegetables, sometimes washing dishes. She always dressed well. There was no other option. In Belarus, when you went out in public you always dressed well, a skirt, stockings, a blouse or sweater, nice shoes. To work in the kitchen, she'd put on an apron. It was a restaurant where they put on shows in the evening. It stayed open all night. She would leave in the morning hours. During the daytime, she began working in houses, cleaning and ironing. She worked in twelve houses a week. Eventually, she stopped working at the restaurant. She earned more in the houses and the hours were better, allowing her to spend more time with her children. After several years of this, she began training in the beauty trade, which she preferred to both.

"When I got here, I promised myself not to suffer in this country. I had suffered so much. Okay, anything else? Bikini line?"

I grimaced. "I don't know."

When she smiled, she looked like a chipmunk. "It's nice," she said. "For your boyfriend." There was a blank where those words stood, but I didn't say that.

Oh, well, what the hell, I thought, since I seem to be trying everything else.

"Okay." By now I knew the drill. I took off my underwear.

She looked. "You never did this before?"

I shook my head. I wasn't looking where she was. Already dreading it.

"How much do you want removed?" she asked.

"I don't know," I said. "How much are you supposed to?"

"You can take off everything or a little on the sides. Here, look." I sat up and looked with her, the two of us staring matter-of-factly between my legs. "Or you can just leave a little strip here. That's what I do."

"Okay," I said, "let's do the little strip."

She gobbed the wax on, then pulled. The pain here was what I'd felt earlier with the legs, only magnified at least a dozen times, dizzying. At first I couldn't believe it. I certainly couldn't speak. The skin afterward was pink and tingling. It also felt weird having a woman's hands moving so matter-of-factly over my private parts.

We were quiet for a while.

When she finished, there was, indeed, just a little strip. "Okay, take that off too," I said. Vera laughed.

Afterward, Vera held up the hand mirror. "Look at that," she said. I sat up and looked. It was a new sight, pink and gray, the curving folds all visible. Vera doused the whole area with powder.

I walked back across the bridge to the bus stop on the other side. I passed a boy, who glanced at me sideways. Then a woman in her fifties did a double take. Passing under the jacaranda, the translucent violet bells littering the ground, leaving the branches bare, I felt sure everyone knew.

twelve

The guy who had kissed her at the party, Diego, had entered Isolde's brainstream. "I can't stop thinking about him," she told me. "I actually wrote to him the other day when I was sitting in the *locutorio*. I looked up his name on a group invitation and sent him an e-mail."

"What did you say?"

She shrugged. "I invited him to meet for coffee or a drink sometime. He didn't write back right away. Then this morning he did. I'll forward you the e-mail. You can tell me what you think."

She actually did send me the e-mail. Avoiding her question, full of prance and seduction, a male ruffling his feathers, it opened:

> "This world was once a fluid haze of light,
> Till toward the centre set the starry tides,
> And eddied into suns, that wheeling cast
> The planets: then the monster, then the man."

Isolde looked up the quote online. It was from Tennyson's "The Princess." So he thinks of me as a princess? she thought. She pressed for a meeting. Diego wrote back another ornate e-mail, then silence, then at her urging, finally relented. "It felt like that," she said. He suggested they meet at a bar downtown. In inimitable detail, as only Isolde could, she told me what had happened.

Diego arrived a bit late, swaggering in his long leather coat, which he obviously thought was very cool. He had faint beer cigarette breath, large features, nose and lips, a cleft in his chin, and a shaded, guarded look, though at the same time his brown eyes, slightly small, were warm. Isolde noticed that his fingernails were clean, as if they'd been cared for. His cool guy behavior was both absurd and delighted her. She pictured kissing him, his mouth, again.

He worked in the music industry, he told her. "But I get bored easily," he said. "Now if I had money, I'd do a lot of crazy shit," he said, "like Howard Hughes kind of shit."

"What did Howard Hughes do?"

"You know, he produced these crazy movies, he was an engineer and flew planes, he broke all the world records for airline speeding." He snickered. "Now that made sense that he had money. But usually it's the wrong guys who have the money. They have it but they don't *do* things with it."

He was looking at her sideways, wary, not entirely looking at her, but musing about her, she could feel it. Something about him made her comfortable. Was it that, despite his whole cool act, he was afraid?

"What about you? What are you up to?"

Isolde, as always, was slightly taken aback. "Oh, I'm working on a project to connect artists around the world," she said.

He seemed amused. "Uh-huh." But seeing as she didn't elaborate, he quickly returned to the subject of himself.

"The music shit's fine. I like music, the weird shit, the stuff no one else likes and that you can never sell, but what I'm really interested in is science."

"Science?"

"Yeah, science is my hobby." He was obviously trying to seduce, his arrogance mixed with innocence. But Isolde was also beginning to think he had a propensity to ramble.

"Hey," she said. "Should we walk a bit?"

He seemed surprised. "Okay," he said.

They began walking toward the Plaza San Martín.

"Do you live around here?" Isolde asked.

"Yeah."

"Where's your apartment?"

"Back that way. It's my parents' place. I moved back in after the crash."

Living with his parents, this surprised her.

They had arrived at the grassy slope that tumbled down from the Plaza San Martín.

"See, here," he said, pointing to a grassy patch. "This is where the first slave market was held." He snickered. "Should we honor the sacred ground?" He sat. She followed suit.

"Anyway, systems theory is my latest thing," he said.

Oh, boy, here we go again, she thought.

"What's that?" she asked.

"It's this idea that everything is organized into systems. Everything, all around us. And there are systems within systems."

"What's an example of a system?" she asked.

"Well, society is a system. So is your brain. Each system has an inertia, meaning a structure that stays the same, though it's also a dynamic thing in constant interaction with everything around it. When a system is stable, it absorbs a disruption, receiving stimuli and readjusting its structure. Of course, this means that systems have these very complicated feedback processes. A whole complex chain of causes and effects is triggered until the system reworks itself into a new stability, which might have been entirely unforeseen by the researcher."

She was letting the images bloom in her brain. "Okay, but does it ever happen that a system can't absorb a disruption?"

"Yeah, sure. When a system is functioning well, it absorbs a disruption. But when it's close to a threshold of instability, a disruption can turn the whole thing around, like the example of the drop that overflows the glass or the revolution of a society."

"And then what happens?"

"Two options. Either the system reconfigures itself entirely, or it ceases to exist."

But Isolde couldn't just go on sitting there, listening. Her impetuousness got in the way. She turned and rolled on top of him.

"Hey, wait a second," Diego said, laughing, "shouldn't I be on top?"

She fell to the ground again.

"Was it that exciting what I said?" he asked.

He leaned over and kissed her. It was a kiss like the one at the party with a lot of tongue. She closed her eyes—deliciousness, the whole world recedes—then opened them again, aware of the tumbling grass, the towering trees of the Plaza San Martín. He had moved downward, was lifting up her shirt. He surprised her now by putting his tongue in her belly button. The whirling world. She reached to touch him, his stomach, chest. He flinched slightly.

"I haven't exercised in two years," he said. "I'm out of shape. I'm going to start."

But his body felt nice to her. They were kissing again. He pulled back for a second and looked at her. Due to the effect of the kiss, that gaze of his, dark and sheltered, had changed. She must have looked different too.

"It's like we're on drugs," he said.

The cars swishing by, the stars coming out. That's what I want, Isolde thought, for him to always look at me like that.

"Why did you kiss me at that party?" she asked.

"I don't know. I just felt like doing it."

He leaned in and kissed her again.

"This is the first sex I've had in years," he said.

"What?"

"Yeah, really."

"You mean this kissing?"

"Yeah. I was involved with this girl. She was there at the party. She really fucked me up."

"Who? Leonarda?"

"Uh-huh. What you don't want to ever do is fall in love. That's what fucks you up. No, no, you want to stay away from that."

thirteen

"Just imagine," Leonarda said, "that we're hunting him down." We were walking again through the Plaza Las Heras. "See, he's there, running. You remember that movie *The Conformist*, when they're hunting Dominique Sanda between the trees? Oh, just picture it, there he is running, scared shitless. I take a shot, not even trying to hit him, just to scare him. But I mean really scare him. The primal fear at the heart of all human beings, reverberating back into the very deep past when they were hunted by predators, giant animals, the fear of being overtaken, killed and eaten. This was before they discovered how to build fires."

She stopped walking to explain this last point to me.

"You see, the fires allowed them to change the dynamic. Predators were afraid of fires, so if the humans stayed near the fire, they could no longer be surprised in the night. The other idea, of course, was to form bands. They began hunting the big predators, bears, lions, in groups. A man was helpless before a large predator, but a group of ten could kill it. You see? Look at books for kids. They're all about tapping into that fear of predators. We still have it. I want to reawaken that fear in him, awaken it to its most acute point."

"But wait," I said, "wasn't he actually already involved in violent combat? Doesn't he know something about this?"

She looked at me full of annoyance. It was as if she'd dropped her rifle right then and there. "He wasn't involved in shit," she said.

I had ruined the moment. I wanted to see her again like a boy, sighting him with her rifle between the trees.

In *Crowds and Power*, Canetti describes the four possible reactions to attack by a predator: fight, flight, paralysis—the pursued hopes to be given up as dead—and metamorphosis. In this last, the being neither flees nor fights, but transforms into something else entirely—Daphne, pursued by Zeus, turns into a tree. Leonarda's tactic was metamorphosis. Sometimes I'd see her in the course of one of our walks transform her entire physiognomy five times. That was also what was riveting. She kept escaping out of your hands, a girl, then a furry creature, a monster, a brightly winged insect, a boy, while I would slink along beside her, the reptile she always said I was. In appearance somewhat frail, compared to me, she could walk for hours.

Those days, I felt lonely when I suspected that she was going back not to her mother's, that witch, but to see the guy Miguel, winner of the prize. Once I even dropped her off at the corner of The Palace of Pigeons and walked on alone, up Las Heras Avenue. It changed at this point, on one side of the street a high wall, the Zoological Gardens, the beasts behind the wall—sometimes you could hear them, a bellow or breathing—no more people coming in and out of stores, just the street beside the wall, the cars swishing by, the wall casting a shadow. It was the end of happiness, the

end of fun. The fun was somewhere else, with her and that guy,
behind other walls. I felt as if the sense of my life had stepped away
from me.

I didn't know if they were sleeping together. I knew that they
were appearing in public together, yet I also knew that appearing to
be sleeping with someone was, for some, supremely more significant than actually doing it.

I'd read in a short book Brian had given me, *Buenos Aires, Daily
Life and Alienation*, that from early on, to the recorded surprise of
visitors, the Argentine aristocracy took on a highly mannered and
sumptuous role only comparable to czarist or Central European
aristocracy in its heyday. For many of these families, the money
itself was already gone. Their lives were dedicated to obscuring this
fact, well-known though it was among people who mattered. Yet
the point was not, in fact, what was known, but what was revealed.
Without revelation, there was no shame. Certain houses, including
The Palace of Pigeons, were designated as suitable for the upper
classes, even though the rents were cheap. Another bulwark against
reputational ruin, even if material ruin had already occurred, was to
be listed in the voluminous tomes of the *Nobiliario del antiguo Vir-
reynato del Río de la Plata*.

The game, while acknowledged by everyone, functioned precisely because the truth was of very little interest to all parties, and
only existed on a much lower rank of prestige than appearance.
Thus, today within certain Argentine social circles, you can discover
prominent couples who, after appearing in public at an art opening
or theater event, then apparently go home together only to part on

the sidewalk in front of one or the other's house, complicitly acknowledging with the standard one-cheek kiss what seems but will never be, before turning and going their separate ways home.

One day, Leonarda asked me to pick her up outside the guy's house. She came out breathless. "You know what the problem is? Without beauty, there's nowhere to hide."

Another day, she told me she was growing a dick. "I always wanted to be a sailor. I have an ontological dick. But now it's really growing."

"It is?" I asked. It was amazing how with her I always half believed.

I couldn't help looking down at her crotch, which she covered quickly with her hands.

"No, no, it's not ready. You have to wait," she said. "He's so excited about it. He wants me to stick it in him."

She would sometimes insinuate that I should come along with her, that we should play with him together, drive him crazy that way. She would talk about his bald head, gleaming, how the orb of his bald head would confront the two "lovely orbs" of my butt. I wasn't at all sure I wanted to go. But then at the last minute, she would flit away anyway.

Finally, one evening, the encounter occurred.

He was in the doorway, bowing, baring his teeth, rabbit-like. His brown eyes actually, surprisingly, a bit simple. He was tall and hairy, except for on his head. You could see the hair bristling up around the neck of his shirt.

He led us inside. Everything about the apartment was well-chosen, masculine, an almost effete choice of masculine items, as if a very good female set designer had been involved. There were bookshelves along all the walls extending nearly to the ceiling. The couch and armchairs were of soft brown cow leather. The desk, in dark wood, was large and sturdy. On it were papers stacked neatly, a row of pipes. The apartment was on the first floor. Before the desk was a window that looked out onto a garden. The view was low, of the grass and the bottom part of bushes. You had to crane a bit to see the sky. The bedroom, a smaller room, was off the living room, its walls also lined with bookshelves. There was a not unpleasant smell of pipe tobacco.

Leonarda was smiling, holding my hand.

Between the leather furniture, armchairs and couches, was a very big, very bright lamp, as you would use on an operating table. I glanced at it. I pictured being placed under that lamp, me and Leonarda, unclothed.

He led us into the kitchen. He had long lower limbs, calves and forearms. He was cooking dinner for us. He was, she had told me, a great chef, among his multiple other accomplishments. On the counter was a large piece of cured ham, stretched on a spit.

"See, look at what Miguel has." Leonarda pointed at the stuck ham. "He's the height of sophistication." She giggled. He looked pleased despite himself, despite even the evident mockery of the comment. "Oh, could we please each have a piece?" she asked, child-like, begging, entirely unnecessarily.

He looked at her with tolerance mixed with delight.

He took a large knife with a wooden handle, too large a knife really for the task at hand, and sawed some pieces off. He handed them to us on little napkins.

"Come," Leonarda said to me, turning, chewing on the meat, "look at the wines."

He had a shelf of wines. Above the cooking stove, high on the wall, was a painted portrait someone had done of him, the great man, gazing out.

They began talking now, just the two of them, sparring, while I looked on.

He turned to me. He had an apron on. "I apologize for speaking in Spanish," he said. "My English is imprecise."

But it wasn't that. They spoke the same language in another sense. That was what he held forth, that they spoke the same language, made the same allusions, literary, historical. In each was perfected the Argentine will toward superiority.

Here, when they were talking, he still had a footing. I could tell, even now, he was gaining on her. He knew more, if only because he'd spent more time alive. Despite Leonarda's bravado, he could still make her nervous. She still admired, respected him, much as she hated herself for it. Yet it was also for that that she was here. She would ask him questions without looking at him, as if he wasn't even worthy of her glance. The more important the question, the more she'd look away or at least feign to look away. You could see that, in fact, it really was a charade; she was looking near enough to catch the movements of his form if not the focused picture.

It seemed that once again the tables had turned. Again, she was mocking him. She had read his books, though she pretended not to have. She knew all the information in them. It was important that, to the degree possible, she knew everything he knew. That he couldn't make an allusion that she wouldn't pick up on. Of course, this wasn't my territory, what they were discussing, Argentine history. So what was my territory here? In short, what the hell was I doing here? The way he looked at me sometimes, it seemed he had the same question.

I suddenly felt confused, as if I'd woken up out of a dream. Why did she want me here at all? For protection? Maybe there was an element of that, but after all, she saw him often enough on her own. I suddenly felt that there was no purpose to my presence at all. I looked around, saw the open window, venue for escape. I could step right out into the garden.

Leonarda saw me looking out at the garden.

"Hey, Daddy," she asked, "can I show Daisy the garden?"

"You aren't allowed to at night," he said, then seeing her exasperated teenage face, "but yes, yes, go."

Leonarda passed by him, brushing her breasts against him, then turned. "Oops," she laughed. One of the buttons of her shirt was open, exposing half a luminous breast.

He smiled but he was too stricken to find it actually funny.

Leonarda and I stepped out through the window, climbing up and over the sill right into the garden. There was a jasmine bush nearby that gave off a dizzying smell—we picked sprigs of it—then a round stretch of grass. We walked across the stretch of grass.

"You were perfect," Leonarda said. "Your behavior was perfect."

"What do you mean?" I asked, gratified to have done well on the one hand.

She shrugged. "I told him all about you. And you were just the way I described."

"What way?" Now I was annoyed. "And why should I be acting any way for him?"

"Not for him. For me, silly." She suddenly looked solemn. "I told him I was in love with you and that would never change." Then, changing the subject, pulling me along by the hand, "I like to call him Daddy," Leonarda said.

Still disgruntled, I didn't answer.

We had come to a dark patch in the garden, along the edge, the tree above thickened with masses of coiling vines, blocking out all the light. Leonarda clutched my arm in the dark. "He could be your daddy too. We could both be his daughters. I asked him and he said that he'd adopt us."

As my eyes adjusted, I saw on a nearby ledge a statue of a little boy, white stone. He was sitting, legs crossed, one foot broken off at the ankle.

I suddenly didn't feel like playing anymore. "Maybe I don't need a daddy. Maybe I even want to have a kid myself one day," I said.

It felt absurd to say it, incongruous, and also as if I was breaking some pact.

But Leonarda, typically, rearranged everything.

"Oh, you could. He could father it. I'm sure he'd do it if I asked him."

Suddenly, I hated the guy, pathetic as he might appear in this recent incarnation. It seemed there was no getting away from him, in which case I thought, yes, he should be punished, let's punish him even further, as much as we can.

"Do you have sex with him?" I asked, wanting and not wanting to know. She'd told me they didn't but I was no longer sure of anything.

Leonarda giggled. "No," she said. "I told you. He's dying to see me naked. It's the only thing he wants."

"But, I mean, are you naked? Do you take off your clothes?"

"I had an image, I had an image," she interrupted. "We would isolate one room in a public place that would be like a cage. We'd put him in there, tied up, chained. It would be like a performance piece. You could throw things at him. He'd be howling. But he would like it too. He would agree to do it, if I asked him. The public could come by and throw things."

She stopped and turned to me. "Can you believe what we've done? The Master Plan is working. It's really working. And it's beautiful, so beautiful."

Two guards appeared, walking swiftly across the grass.

"Have you lost something?" the first one asked.

"Who are you?" the second one said abruptly.

"We're friends of Miguel's," Leonarda said. "And yes, I have lost something." She burst into tears. "My diamond engagement ring." Grabbing my hand, she ran with me across the grass to the window of his apartment where, like children, we tumbled inside.

"What happened?" Miguel asked, as we clambered in. He was still at the stove.

"Oh, nothing," Leonarda said, "those stupid guards. Okay, Daddy, we have to go. Come, come," she said to me, again brushing her breasts against him as she passed, taking my hand and leading me out the door.

"What about dinner?" we heard him call.

But we were already gone.

fourteen

Despite my better judgment, it seemed this hunting metaphor was going to my head. It was a September evening, spring, all the flowering trees in bloom. As there was no food in the house, I went to the grocery store. Lugging the bags home, I pictured that I was dragging an animal carcass. I suddenly felt ravenous. Had I been ravenous before? Just a block or two past the supermarket, I stopped on the sidewalk, juggling one bag in my arm, the other between my legs, and tore open the cheese package. I sunk my teeth in, then threw it, half bitten, back in the bag. Still ravenous a few blocks later, I stopped again and tore open the ham, stuffing a whole wad in my mouth.

I met Gabriel in the foyer of my building.

"Come upstairs with me," I said.

He looked good, in his gigolo mode, tight striped T-shirt and jeans.

"I just came from the doctor," Gabriel said, following me in down the tiled hall of my apartment.

"Really? Are you all right?"

"Yeah, just a checkup." He smiled. "A new guy. When I arrived, he went into the bathroom and changed into a white coat. Crazy.

He just wanted me to take my clothes off and get down on all fours while he examined me. That was it. A hundred pesos."

"He did nothing?"

"No, well, I mean, he felt my balls and put his finger in my butt, but he didn't even touch himself."

Gabriel did a little dance step. "Hey, let's have some wine."

We were in the kitchen. A winged cockroach flew through. "Aah, shit!" He ducked. "You live with that shit?"

He danced around again, as I poured out the wine.

"This is what I'm learning," Gabriel said. "The problem is that people think sex is one thing. Like you have to figure it out or something. When it's not. It can be anything. Whatever you want it to be.

"I mean, just look at the johns. They really know what they want. There was this guy— Oh, wow, that's right"—his face opened up—"there was this guy in my elementary school. You know what he did? He would get us to come into the bathroom. He was older, like thirteen or fourteen, we were nine or so. He'd be lying there on the ground with his arms out, palms up, and he'd get us to step on the palms of his hands with our bare feet. He had his eyes closed. Then he would pay us, three pesos."

I had handed him a glass of wine. "Isn't that awesome?"

"Yeah, great scene."

"That's what I admire. That guy knew exactly what he wanted."

He wiggled his butt a bit more, dancing. "I can't help it," he said. "I feel like I have a motor in my butt. Oh, but wait—" He stopped moving. "How's the hunt going?"

"Good," I said. "It seems we've got him cornered."

"Are you serious? The great man?"

I nodded. "He's enthralled with her. You should see the way he acts. Like he puts an apron on and cooks for us."

"Really?" Gabriel paused. He seemed to be marveling. "Now, I'd like to see *that*."

fifteen

Isolde woke, heart pounding, thinking of Diego. She had to see him, it couldn't wait. They'd met a few times since the time they'd kissed on the grassy slope of the Plaza San Martín, meetings that had been both tantalizing and frustrating. There had been people around. They'd only had a moment. Once, in a cab, on the way home from a dinner with a group of people, he'd lifted up her skirt and moved his fingers up her thigh, then licked both her nostrils. Impulsive, she'd put her hand on his crotch, too soon, it was clear. "Whoa," he'd said, moving away.

The way to reach Diego was through e-mail. You were much more likely to get a response than if you called. It was nine in the morning, early for Buenos Aires. Isolde bypassed her regular café and went directly to the *locutorio* on the corner. She'd written him yesterday, frustrated. It would be different if there were something blocking them being together, like he was married or even just with someone, but that was not the case. She checked her e-mail. He hadn't answered.

The *locutorio* was gradually filling up. There was a boy crouched over a computer, watching YouTube. There was a woman in a phone booth, not even talking, just fixing her makeup in the mirror there. A student with a washed-out look on her face was writing a paper.

A man sitting in front of a computer was talking nonstop on his cell phone. This seemed to be his office. He had papers taped up all around his cubicle. A row of four kids, nine or ten years old, were sitting side by side playing video games. A woman entered, looking rushed. She glanced over her shoulder. Isolde watched her. Wasn't it clear to everyone that she was having an affair? She went into a phone booth and made a quick call, all the while glancing furtively around.

Isolde read her e-mails. Friends from Austria were getting married, having babies, changing jobs. She would still receive invitations to their events, and even to the events of people from college she hadn't seen in years. One guy, who had briefly been a boyfriend of hers, had visited Buenos Aires five months ago. "But what are you doing here?" he'd asked. "You're not doing anything!" he'd concluded with some derision. Now she thought of them all thinking of her like that, in Buenos Aires doing nothing. Their lives were going on and what about her? But she wasn't necessarily jealous of her friends. Except maybe for one, who had married a British lawyer and moved to Sussex, they were all living normal lives, in Austrian cities and towns. In Uruguay last year, when she'd first arrived, she'd had a glimpse of something else for herself, something different, glowing. It was that glimpse that she was holding on to.

Or was she? What did Diego have to do with that glimpse? Unlike Alfonso, he wasn't rich or upper class, though he had friends in those circles. He'd grown up outside the city of Buenos Aires. He was smart and liked to play the maverick, the outsider, hiding that he was actually quite conventional at heart. He certainly didn't want to marry—he had a whole long anti-marriage discourse—though surely, eventually, he would marry, still reluctantly, a much younger wife, and have a few children. But that was a long way off, ten years or so. By then, Isolde would be too old to have children. No, this choice of hers was not coherent with any of her plans. Only it didn't feel like a choice, but a compulsion. Isolde felt that she would do anything for those moments when Diego looked at her with warmth, like that day on the grassy slope, kissed her as he had. These days, when she woke in the morning, facing another day when he wouldn't write or call, the loneliness stretched out. She felt that she loved him. Without a doubt, he had disrupted her system. Granted that the stability of Isolde's system was probably a bit wobblier than most.

An old man came into the *locutorio* with some papers in his hand that needed to be typed out. He asked for help using the computer. A young woman was screaming on the phone, really screaming at her father. This was clear because she kept saying, "Papa!" She came out of the cubicle, her face streaming with tears. The guy at the cash register watched her, curious, deadpan. It began raining outside, that kind of Buenos Aires rain that made the whole sky turn dark. You'd think it was nighttime when it was only noon. Isolde looked up. Had the day passed already? It wouldn't be the first time that she'd spent six hours here. But no, it was only noon.

She checked the cultural pages of the Argentine newspapers online, browsed some opera websites. What if he never wrote her again, disappeared entirely? She pictured a blank world, desolate, without him.

In that moment, Diego replied. "Sure, we can meet," he said, as if it were entirely casual, something that happened every day. He proposed another downtown bar, again near the Plaza San Martín. Yes, Isolde thought, then we can go back and lie on the grass. That patch of grass had become enchanted ground in her mind.

She hurriedly left the *locutorio* and went home, so as to figure out what to wear. Until she had decided, it would be impossible to go on with the rest of her day.

"I like that idea, it's a Kafka idea, that there's been a misunderstanding and that misunderstanding is going to ruin your life," Diego said. They were sitting in the window of the bar, facing the street.

Isolde was wearing a peach-colored blouse, which the waitress had admired. There were certain days like this when people were always admiring and commenting on her clothes, as a way to articulate what was in fact a larger impression, of sunniness, freshness.

Now she furrowed her brow. "What do you mean, there's been a misunderstanding?"

Diego shook his head. "Just that, there's been a misunderstanding. There's always a misunderstanding."

But then he was kissing her again, those deep tongue kisses that someone else might have found disgusting, but she loved.

"Can we go somewhere?" He lived with his parents and she wasn't allowed to have people at her apartment. Though she had decided that, if it was the only option, today she would break the rule.

He laughed at her eagerness. "Okay, okay. Take it easy. Finish your drink."

Diego's hair had grown longer. On the one hand, he looked shaggier than ever. On the other, he had a white leather bag, utterly unnecessary fingerless gloves, all these dandyish accoutrements. He'd stopped smoking all the time like before because it was making him sick and now just had the coveted few. Once outside, he lit a cigarette.

He led her down the street just a few blocks away to a hotel *transitorio*, or *telo*. Isolde had heard about these places—they were everywhere throughout the city—where you could go to have sex, paying by the hour. The place was called The Three Princes. They stepped inside. There was a dark red patterned carpet on the floor and a person in a booth walled in by glass. Facing the booth was a screen with different room numbers on it. You could press a number and an image would appear of the corresponding room. Diego pressed a few of the numbers and the images appeared: the Empire State Building, the Taj Mahal.

"Which one do you like?" he asked.

She chose the jungle room. They turned to the glass booth. Diego paid and ordered three beers.

"Three?" she asked.

"Yeah, just in case," he said. He seemed nervous.

They took the elevator upstairs without touching, then walked down the hall to room number 48. Just inside the door was a plant

with dark red and green leaves on a little table, lit by a lamp overhead. The walls were covered with painted leaves and animals. The
bedspread had tiger stripes, the chairs spots. Animal print was a
very common wardrobe choice among Argentine women, Isolde
had noticed, especially among a certain kind of celebrity crowd.
Isolde used to wear it too sometimes before arriving, but since had
stopped, not wanting to give off a cheapish air. There was a jungle
swing and a large TV playing porn, where a guy with an enormous
dick was getting a blow job.

"I don't like that," Diego said, and turned it off.

Isolde felt confused by what he wanted. Last time, when they
were kissing she worried she'd been too proactive, excited. Maybe
she should hold off, let him make the moves.

He waved his hand in her direction. "Take off your clothes,"
he said.

He took off his clothes as well. She liked the way the hair was
dispersed on his body, a nice amount everywhere, except for his
lower legs, which were nearly hairless.

Then, all at once, he was down on his knees on the floor, licking
her with his very large tongue. She was at the edge of the bed. "It's
like a flower," he murmured and went on licking. The men she'd
been with recently had hardly even touched her, a few jerks with
two fingers, and here he was licking. He seemed to like doing this
very much. First lifting her head to watch, she then dropped it and
let him.

At one point, he pulled her feet over her head, as if she were a
child, a baby, and licked her asshole. She was startled. No one had

ever done this to her before. Although the rest of the encounter was nice as well—he was tentative at first, only gradually letting her touch him—this became the part she went over and over in her head. For a long time after that, at random moments throughout the day, she would feel the touch of his tongue there. It was like an imprint, something primitive. He had touched deep inside her. She would do anything to be touched like that by him again.

When they came back downstairs, there was a sea of people waiting, a long line leading up to the glass booth, which spread out through the lobby, couples of all ages, some holding hands, some standing separate, more like strangers, their faces all registering divergent motives, the bleary-eyed, the frightened, the pros— for the young couple holding hands, it would be their first time. The vision veered between that of a group of individuals, each with a heart throbbing, a particular way of doing his or her hair, to a collection of types—there was something didactic in the bright light—representing the various ages, walks, intentions of humanity. The line spilled out onto the sidewalk, trailing down it to one side.

Isolde and Diego walked up the street. Except for a few places here and there, a bar, a restaurant, probably a brothel, the downtown streets were deserted. They came upon a kiosk, lit up, and bought bottled water, then arrived at the Plaza San Martín. The trees were towering, the figures below looking minuscule.

They crossed the street and entered the park. He held out his arm and she took it.

"Hey, look at this. This is my favorite statue." It was called

Doubt, a present from the French, and featured two figures. One, a young man, was sitting on the ground with a worried expression. An older, toothless man was leaning in, whispering in the young man's ear and smiling. Diego snickered. "Just look at the slimy, older guy," he said.

Behind them in the park, people shuffled on the benches, either homeless people sleeping or couples making out, it was too dark to see. They passed a monumental statue, military figures with their chests flung out.

"It's like I feel like Alexander the Great," he said. "But I don't see the Empire."

Isolde laughed. "Maybe you have to build the Empire."

"Yeah, well, I'm too lazy for that."

They headed down the hill, on one side ghostly downtown buildings, on the other, the dark, cool grass of the park.

"According to quantum physics," Diego said, "you can't locate an object in space. All you can do is point at a cloud of probable places where it could be. An electron is not in a certain spot, but a little bit smeared everywhere."

"I don't get it."

"Okay, take this example. You're walking down a crowded street, like Florida, you know it, the pedestrian street right back there, people turn, dodge, shift position, so they won't hit you. They accommodate themselves so as not to run into one another. In every next moment, a person will be somewhere different, on a different part of the street, walking, or stepping into a car. This is similar to the way the Greeks talked about potentiality. The next few steps could take you to different places. Or, if you're running, the whole time you're running, you're realizing possibilities. We ourselves are like projections into the future, not certainties, but waves of probabilities. Beings in a potential state, a little bit everywhere. At any moment, we could do this or that."

sixteen

Unlike animals, plants are immobile and can't seek out sexual partners for reproduction, so they must devise other ways. In his book *The Intelligence of Flowers*, Maeterlinck writes beautifully about the plight of plants, condemned by their roots to stay fixed in one place. Consequently, among all living beings, flowers or the reproductive structures of plants are the most varied physically and possess the greatest diversity of reproductive strategies. Over eighty-five percent of flowering plants are hermaphroditic. Some have both male and female flowers, while others, like the *Echinopsis spachiana*, have bisexual flowers, otherwise known as perfect or complete flowers, possessing both male and female sexual organs, the pollen-producing stamen, or male part, and the seed-producing carpels, or female part. Many of these plants are self-fertile, the male parts pollinating the female parts of the same flower. Others have self-incompatibility clauses that make this impossible and promote outcrossing. Some plants undergo what is called sex-switching, expressing sexual difference at different stages of growth. In the case of the *Arisaema triphyllum*, the plant expresses a multitude of sexual conditions in the course of its lifetime, from nonsexual juvenile plants to young all-male plants, to plants with a mix of male and female flowers to large plants with mostly female flowers.

Miguel was gone, traveling. He had lent Leonarda his house. She invited me over.

I entered the lobby, passing by the doorman, the sleek wood floors, the interior pillars, a quiet view of the back garden. I rang the bell. I heard something and felt that she'd been waiting for me behind the door.

She opened the door. She was dressed in men's pants and a button-down shirt. She had a mustache on. Then she was hiding behind the door.

"Wait, wait, let me see," I said. She had turned her face to the wall. When I stepped nearer, she ran, still hiding her face. She went into the bathroom and closed the door.

"I'm taking it off," she said.

"No, no, don't take it off. I want to see you."

I waited in the hall. I barely breathed. I thought I could hear her breathing too, on the other side of the bathroom door.

"Please, Leo," I said, "I want to see you."

But I didn't want to insist too much. She was quiet. A few minutes passed. Then I heard her opening the bathroom door. She came out again with the mustache still on. She looked different. In her proud mode, boyish, standing straight. In those minutes in the bathroom, she had allowed the transformation to occur. Knowing her, I was afraid that something else would happen. She would change again. I didn't want to move, to do anything that would make her change again. She stepped near and pressed me against the wall. She kissed me. I could feel her breasts, full and round. But I could also feel as she pressed against me that she had a dick in her pants.

She led me through the living room past the leather furniture and the operating lamp to the bed. She took off my clothes and had me lie down. I had imagined this moment many times and finally it was occurring. She licked me, delicately at first, like a cat. Then she pulled the mustache off and began to really lick, applying pressure with her teeth and tongue.

I was so thrilled I couldn't think.

"See," she said afterward, lifting her head, "I don't need a dick." Her face was flushed with triumph. "What can I bring you?"

She brought me some juice, then went into the bathroom and changed her clothes, putting on makeup and perfume, coming out in a little pink T-shirt dress that reached mid-thigh. I was sitting up on the edge of the bed. She was girly, flirty. "Now I'm going to cook," she said.

These visits made me dizzy. The thrill was that she combined everything, girl, boy, youth. The one thing she was not was mature.

The next visit, I asked if I could lick her this time.

"Okay," she said. She seemed nervous. She went to wash first, then came out and sat under the lamp. She had shaved. I could see the line of shaved hair going down from her belly button, on her pussy that glistening veil of snail trail substance. She tasted bitter, not in an unpleasant way. Her breasts were heavy, strong and nervous, pressing against her T-shirt.

I would go back to my house to sleep and wake in the night,

feeling disoriented. Not so much about where I was, which city, though that would happen too, than a deeper confusion inside my brain. It was as if my conception of the human adventure had changed. The things I had held to be important, at the center of my life, suddenly seemed insignificant, bits of stray matter swirling around. I felt that I needed to find new ideas, new ways of conceiving of a life, any life, including my own. I would find these ideas not within myself, but outside. And I would have to look beyond the systems I was used to, to seek out, insist on, disruption.

Leonarda showed me what she'd been doing, acts of private vandalism throughout his house. She had mixed the colognes in the bathroom, opened a bottle of what she assured me was very good wine and half filled it with a bottle that was mediocre. She had been shifting paintings, objects, furniture slightly to the left, placing everything, however slightly, awry.

Certain figures in Buenos Aires are known to have important libraries. If you need a book, you can find a friend who has a friend who knows this guy who probably has it. Then you can hope to arrange an introduction. These figures with the marvelous libraries are often happy to lend books—it is, after all, part of their prestige. They rarely ever ask for a book back directly, too gross a gesture. Rather, if the book is not returned, they find ways of securing it, sending envoys who insinuate themselves into your house and slip the book off your shelf when your back is turned.

Miguel was the possessor of one of these famous libraries. Leonarda had been scrutinizing his books. She showed me the way he made comments as he read, underlined things. For her part, she had

been making comments on his comments, disparaging, mocking re-
marks or suggestions for further reading, there was something he
hadn't understood. The next time, she showed me some love letters
from a woman, where she'd done the same, put commentary in the
margins, made grammatical corrections.

Must youth be bound up with evil? What was not clear to me
was to what degree Leonarda's evilness was real and to what degree
an affectation, a generative force to make something happen. And
what about me? Was I drawn to this evilness, even thrilled by it? I
had actually never considered being evil before. New terrains were
opening all around me.

Little by little, I was becoming aware of the magnitude of her
target. It seemed to have grown, and taken on all kinds of shadowy
significance, like those deep water beasts on whose hides crusta-
ceans accrue to the point where the actual animal disappears from
view. Sometimes, it seemed that we were moving in this deep water
light, luminous and murky at the same time, an occasional ray cutting through. Did she sense the same murkiness? She of the million
synapses firing at once. Could I be aware of something she wasn't?

At other times, it seemed that the light was firmly on, maybe
even too bright. She kept that clinical operating-table light on all
the time. It was as if she were preparing for some awful surgery,
laying out her shiny tools.

"Can we turn that off, please?" I asked one day.

She shrugged. "Sure"—flicking it off—"why?"

With it off, I felt better, as if he was less present, more gone.
Even though, of course, he was everywhere.

One night when I came over, she was crying.

"What is it?" I asked.

She had her terribly exposed look. "Sometimes I just feel so alone."

"Maybe you should leave here," I said. "Do you want to come stay with me?"

"No, no, it's not that. It's that sometimes I feel that if I were arrested, accused of some terrible crime, no one around would defend me. No one would stand up for me, say to the cops: 'You're fucking crazy, she didn't do it.'"

"Wouldn't your family?"

"No, they'd think I'd done it." She looked miserable. She waited. "I was thinking maybe you might be the one, the only one, who would vouch for me. But I'm not even sure of that."

She looked away, waiting.

I paused too long. Would I stand up for her? Of course I would want to defend her. But would I actually believe she hadn't done what she'd been accused of? Wouldn't I too have a doubt?

"I would, of course I would," I said.

She turned on me fiercely. "No, you wouldn't." Then firmly and more calmly, "Don't lie. The worst thing you could do is lie about it."

The rest of the night she was quiet.

No matter what, in my mind, one thing was certain. I wanted to be with her. I dreamed I was in bed with a woman with full round breasts, who suddenly sat up, revealing her dick, which she put inside me. I understood then too that this was what I wanted.

There was something here that expressed the pinnacle of my desire. I wanted both to be with that girl and to be that girl. She was both the thing I desired and the model.

The dream stayed in my mind as an image of fulfillment, but I was not fulfilled. I walked all over the city, restless, at all hours, to exhaust myself. The smell of the streets, still crowded with young people at three, four in the morning, excited and upset me. I remembered my earlier walks, the way a pall had hung over everything. Now, on the contrary, I felt that I was surrounded by endless combinations of unfamiliar ideas and forms, if only I could seize them.

seventeen

The vine crept in the window. The water ran down the wall in a sheen. I lay on the floor. If I lay there quietly, I would feel something in my chest, a kind of pressure. At first it was painful. Then it gave way. The place was very quiet. I could hear the sounds of water running in the pipes. I pictured water being pumped up from the Río de la Plata, purified, running through all the pipes of the city. Next I pictured the complex of underground streams, the filthy dark water, having been reoriented, sloshing beneath the streets I knew. But I was tired. I wanted to rest. My mind, so excited, wanted to think about nothing, or to only see the same thing over and over again. I let it drift until I saw the water farther out, the empty gray sea, the monotonous lilt of waves, the beautiful regularity of their irregularity, lapping, endlessly, lap, lap, lap.

I must have dozed off. The doorbell, for what it was, a scratchy insect sound more than a bell, woke me. Gabriel was outside.

"What are you doing?" he asked.

"Nothing. Just resting."

He seemed to look at me more closely. "Are you all right?"

"Yeah, just tired."

For the first time, I didn't really feel like telling him what was going on. I was exhausted and there was too much to tell. But also, I felt somewhere a gnawing feeling, that if I told him what I'd been up to, this time he wouldn't approve. Basically, because he would think my mind was not free. It was true, my mind was *not* free.

"Is there such a thing as feeling *too* alive?" I asked. "In medical terms, like, I don't know, what would you call that? Hyperactive, overstimulated?"

He laughed a little. "Those two states exist. You sure you're fine?"

"Yeah, yeah." My phone was ringing. Shit—Isolde.

I arrived late to my lunch meeting with Isolde. She was looking smooth, impeccable, in close-fitting knee-length khaki pants, a white blouse, her blondness. But she was distressed.

"I thought you'd never come," she said.

She didn't want to eat. Was it because she was dieting? I knew that was an interest of hers. I ordered something myself. Only then did it occur to me that she might not have money, difficult as it was to believe with her sitting there looking as she did, expensive in every way. I offered to invite her for lunch. She flushed for a second, then agreed. She ordered the salmon, "with sparkling water, please, that's sparkling, remember." In restaurants she always behaved like one of the entitled, even now, when in despair. But this self-control on her part was highly unusual. It lasted a few moments, then everything tumbled out.

"Diego's disappeared. It's been weeks now that he hasn't answered my e-mails or calls. I don't have any money. I really can't ask my parents again. I know they can't send me anything more."

Bit by bit, she had had to cut back on what were to her basic things: manicures, pedicures, waxing. She had bought a nail kit and a waxing kit. She was now waxing herself. The nails were okay. She held out a hand. She had done them over and over and over again, looking online for instructions until she'd got them right. Though I didn't know a lot about manicures, they looked pretty near perfect to me. The waxing was painful. She'd burnt herself, then left the wax on so long it turned brittle and was almost impossible to pull off. All the same, after several tries, she had managed to give herself a real bikini wax. This included the back.

"What do you mean, the back?"

"The back, the butt. I think it's important." She was serious, stoic, having stopped crying now. Her near plumpness, sometimes invisible, seemed in this moment very touching. The main thing she was worried about, she said, was her hair.

She had wanted at least to keep dyeing it professionally. She was afraid that that too she would have to stop. And then what? Do a home job? She had a horror of how that would look, cheap, above all. Comparatively, eating in restaurants was of the least importance. She could always eat at home.

"What about work?" I asked. "What's happening on that front?" Since I'd met her, she'd been looking around. "Could you work in a bank again, at least for now?"

She had had an interview with an Austrian company. Her qualifications were bizarre, at once too many and too few. The interviewer ended up inviting her out. He wanted to get to know her better. They went to a party at the Italian embassy that very evening. Isolde knew she shouldn't have said yes, if she was actually interested in a job. And anyway, aren't you always supposed to say you have a previous engagement? But she wanted to go. After that, she didn't hear from him again. She knew this was her problem. She appeared too easy. Wasn't that the worst thing for a woman to be? But she couldn't help it. She was simply incapable of biding her time.

I offered her some money, what I had in my wallet, which she took as we parted. "Good, good," she said. "Thank you." She walked away, shoulders back, by the looks of it proudly, although I suspected she was crying again as she turned.

She told me later how she'd stared out the window on the taxi ride home. Hideous city, horribly loud. Dogs barking frantically, both near and far away. It seems that someone is torturing these dogs. There's no other explanation. The grinding sound of traffic, much louder than in other cities, right here, against your ear. The buses heaving, huffing. What has happened to the mufflers, the concept of mufflers? The mufflers in this city all worn out, badly made to begin with. People sit out and dine on the street, screaming at each other above the traffic. It doesn't seem to bother them. They always scream anyway. Argentines scream. At a table full of them, they're all screaming at once. Each one screams his or her own thing, cutting off the other midway. No one ever hears what the other person said. It doesn't matter. The farce of it. The unceasing, bantering show, tears and reclamations. Nobody actually even understands entirely why the other person's crying. Nor does it matter. Hateful, melodramatic race, with their Italian inheritance. People reaching out to strangle each other in restaurants. Another version of the same, old women meeting for tea and repeating over and over exactly the same thing. It's the form, not the content, that it's all about. The endlessly boringly repetitive hours spent at lunches, barbecues, birthdays. The absolute sacralization of birthdays. Three hours attendance is the minimum, five is expected. Six hours in the company of the same people. Everyone gets sick of everyone else. Yet nobody knows when to stop, leave. The long goodbyes. It takes at least an hour. You go around to everyone, one by one, strike up a last conversation, repeat most of the things you've already said, exchange kisses, make plans, open an entirely new conversation, which means you have to turn back, explain yourself, linger, repeat things again, kiss again. By the end, everyone wants to kill each other. They go home in cars, taxis, buses, depleted, hating humanity. The following evening there's a similar event. All the same people will be there.

Sometimes Isolde would feel a kind of Third World revulsion. The streets of Buenos Aires, in certain architectural zones, were like Paris, as everyone said. But all the same, let's admit it, there was a seedy edge. You couldn't forget the hours when the city was scuttling with *cartonero* figures, sifting through the garbage, their hands touching everything, mothers holding small children defecating in the street. One day, Isolde had seen human feces in the subway. In the wealthy Barrio Norte, where she lived, all this was almost invisible, but someone like Isolde was sensitive, she knew it was there. Anyone who'd been to Europe could feel the seediness. It was a down-and-out Paris, a northern zone Paris, taken over by African and Arab immigration. Was this her fate? To live not in Paris, but a seedy simulation? Part of her revolted. When she thought about returning to Europe now, she never thought about returning to the Austrian town where she was from. Her fantasies were about London, of falling in love and having a British family. The illusion was proving more and more complete. She thought of herself as upper class.

Back at home, the cleaning woman, Claudia, was there. The owners of the apartment paid her wages, a common Argentine arrangement. A "rental" came with cleaning services. Claudia eyed Isolde. Isolde felt that she was always eyeing her. Isolde knew little about her, except that she was from the north, Salta, which meant that she spoke with a peculiar accent. Isolde had images of colonial houses, humidity, jungle heat. Once Claudia had missed a week, returning to Salta, because her father had been sick. Claudia was probably Isolde's age, maybe a bit older. She had a funny way of mumbling everything she said, so that sometimes Isolde would get frankly irritated. She'd even told her.

"Look, I'm foreign. I won't understand unless you speak clearly."

But then she began to think that a lot of the time Claudia was just talking to herself. Or at least didn't care if Isolde heard. No matter what, she didn't want to complain. The way Claudia worked was incomparable. Never had Isolde lived anywhere so clean.

As she walked through the apartment, Isolde turned on the lights. Light, light, she needed light. She went into her bedroom and closed the door. Sitting down on her bed, she checked her cell phone in case a message or a call had come in she hadn't heard. Nothing. Loneliness overtook her. It sunk deep inside her, into her bones, as damp weather can. Or it felt like a gray box. She was shut inside. When people spoke about the pleasures of melancholy, she didn't understand it. There was no pleasure here. The loneliness sunk further. It chilled her chest. She felt that she had been alone her whole life. No one had ever actually come near.

She thought with longing of a past she hadn't had, a house full of people and bounding dogs. She saw the dim wet house of her childhood, her mother's shabby attempts at glamour. Her mother had valued glamour too, but had had neither the means nor the exposure to the vision to make it a reality in her home.

Isolde did have a vision. Or at least she had had one. What had happened? The obsession with Diego had entirely derailed her. It was as if she had been on a fleeting silver train, the TGV streaking through the French countryside, and suddenly, instead of getting off at her proposed destination, against all her carefully laid plans, had disembarked at a dingy stop. It looked okay from the outside, like most of those station stops in the French countryside, with petunias in the flower boxes, humble but clean, only in this case what she found, when she went around the corner of the station building, was something else. A run-down house, filth collecting on the walls. The people who lived there had gray faces, their clothes looked greasy. They had no sense at all of glamour or beauty, no urge toward these things, no understanding even of the words. Isolde was meant to live here. Her destiny, it had been decided, was among them, cleaning, cooking, scraping the garden to grow what little they could. The soil in this particular patch was not very fertile. Though she might fight against it, time would tell. Her hair would lose its sheen, go back to dishwater blond. From the work and malnutrition, her skin would go gray, slowly, never maybe entirely as gray as that of the others, but still. At first, scrubbing the house vigorously—she couldn't bear to live in a filthy place—she would gradually desist, it was too much work and what did it matter? There was no one to see. Dirt would begin to collect again on the walls.

Isolde heard Claudia leaving. She felt scared. She went back out into the kitchen. No one. She couldn't stay here. She had to go out.

She walked down the hill to the grassy stretch beside the museum, buying a newspaper on the way. The lilt of spring was settling into summer, at the height of which the days would be sweltering, people trying to move as little as possible, their clothes, when they did, dark with humidity. Beginning with the holidays and through the months of January and February, whoever could would find a means of escape, to the gray-sanded wind-beaten beaches of Argentina, where the water was choppy and cold or, for the flusher, the more golden ones of Uruguay and, for the very few, the pristine paradisiacal white stretches of Brazil. But not yet. It was still early December, the spring flowers drooping and falling from the trees, everyone beginning to shed their clothes. People took to the parks with even more abandon, in couples, groups, families, flinging themselves down on the grass.

The lack of solitary figures pointed up Isolde's loneliness to her. She sat down on a bench and tried to absorb herself in her newspaper, looking for an interesting cultural event. It would have to be something free, like a gallery opening. Next she would have to summon cheer in her voice, pick up her phone and make some calls. "Hellooo, would you like to join me this evening . . ." She thought for a moment. No, she couldn't do it. She let the paper drop in her hand. But she also couldn't return to her apartment, not yet at least. What then? After sitting for a while, she came up with a plan. There was a little cheap restaurant tucked into a side street not far from her house, where you could have a steak and a glass of house wine for ten pesos. She'd eat dinner there. It would be all right, she was sure not to be seen.

eighteen

I was walking along the wall that surrounds Chacarita, the municipal cemetery. I liked this walk. Usually I came here later in the day, around dusk, and walked under the brown light of the lamps. But on this particular day, the sun was still high. The wall cast a delicious cool shade. Animals and people rested in its shelter. Street kids played alongside it in the grass. Occasionally, a street dog crossed my path, trotting busily or loitering, the Buenos Aires street dogs like street dogs everywhere, mutt mixes, fox-like, on the small side, with German shepherd coloring.

I crossed the railroad track and, farther on, where the wall curved, glanced down to discover a flattened dog head, ear, eye, muzzle, all impeccably preserved, only half an inch thick. A pace or so away was the more mangled body.

I walked on, and about a hundred meters ahead, as I was taking the next curve in the wall, I saw a live street dog, unusually large, about three times the size of the standard street doglets, his German shepherd traits more pronounced, only something was wrong with him. He was missing all his fur, except for on his head and around his feet. Instead, the surface of his body was smooth dark gray skin. He was browsing through the garbage on the grass island between the two sides of the road. He shoved at a garbage bag with his nose, glanced up, saw me and headed my way, trotting at a diagonal care-lessly through traffic.

I looked around. No one, nothing. The sidewalk on my side was entirely empty. There was no other explanation—he was coming for me. I began to walk quickly, looking over my shoulder. He was approaching from the traffic side. On my other side was the wall. What to do? Scale the wall? At least with a human being, you could talk, try to seduce or scare him with your words.

The dog had crossed the street and was coming up behind me, trotting. I was now covered in sweat. I was being pursued by an unscrupulous animal. I imagined the murder scene. He'd leap at me, knock me over—he was big enough—knock me out, start eating at my head, then slowly rummage down through the rest of my body, eating at his leisure. Would anyone see? There were hardly any cars passing. The sound of his breath, his footsteps ceased. Was he poised to attack? Would he spring? I stiffened, stopped breathing, prepar-ing myself too. When nothing happened, I glanced back.

The dog had indeed paused. He was looking at me, waiting. As if coming to a decision, he turned and trotted back across the street the other way. He'd decided to spare me this time.

Miguel was back.

"Okay," Leonarda said. "Now I want to do something real."

"Like what?" I asked.

We were standing on the street outside his house, cars parked in front of us. Her look was elated.

"I want to put a virus in his brain," she said. "I want to make him ill, very ill. Will you help me?"

The proposition was so drastic, a crack opened in my vision. I saw Roman Coliseum entertainments, Francis Bacon scenes, a carcass placed on furniture in the center of a room.

At the same time, I pictured myself shouting, again this other register, high drama, "Hold, hold, enough!"

We pranced in together, paraded, danced, breezing past the doorman—of course he knew her—having just made out together against the wall across the street, everything a provocation, childish, yes, adolescent.

The floor had just been polished. I slipped. We giggled. We skated. There was a fat pillar. We twirled around it. His door was behind the pillar. There was a little grate on it.

"Hide, hide," she said.

I hid behind the pillar. He was expecting her, not the two of us. She was changing postures by the minute, now the little girl. She rang the bell. He opened the door. I heard the murmur of his voice, deep, delighted.

"Listen, Daddy," she said. "I have a surprise." I stepped from behind the pillar. "Ta-dah!" she said.

I can't imagine he was happy. Of course he wanted her alone, to do what he would with her. But he remained composed. Or maybe she had also fed him thoughts about the three of us, his head crawling like mine with peculiar erotic scenes. I stepped forward and bowed very low. He bowed in response.

Inside, his desk by the window with its row of pipes, the

operating-table lamp, the soft leather couch beneath it. Okay, so the guy had pretentious taste, but you had to admit his objects were nice. Did anybody ever come to appreciate them? The place gave off a solitary air, all dressed up and nowhere to go. The kitchen with that piece of pig on a stick.

We were dancing, twirling. It was a hot day, but cool inside, the AC on. The great man looked down at us from the portrait above, still the prizewinner in that likeness, as yet minus his present humiliation.

We were sitting at the kitchen table, waiting for our food. The great man was meek, humble, shuffling, again with his apron on, again serving us. At the specter of this, I suddenly felt sorry. "Come," I said, "don't you want to sit with us?"

His cringe was accompanied by a laugh, showing the otherwise invisible stained teeth. Suddenly, I felt a sort of horror. What had we done to him?

But the next moment, he was standing upright, with a saber. I remembered the dog coming after me. Was it possible that I had misunderstood everything? They were in this together, I was the prey?

"Leo," I said. "Leo." Urgently.

I needed to catch her eye. She looked at me, clutched my hand and laughed. That's right, we were together, doing this together. It wasn't a saber, but a knife. He was cutting the ham again, serving us ham. Now he had a corkscrew, he was opening a bottle of wine, telling us about the vineyard, the year, in his deep, melodious radio voice. She lifted her chin, her nose, tasted. She was trying to learn the art of wine-tasting, this, yes, she admired in him and wanted to learn. The little girl now for a moment the snobby, sophisticated woman. She tried to make her neck long. She had confessed once to me that she feared her neck was short. He watched, breathless, would she like it?

Oh, dear, her nose was twitching, what did it mean? Distaste? Disgust? His eyes were on her. She quivered a bit, her entire head on her neck quivering, then looked at him very seriously, gave a dry stern nod and took a second sip—she liked it! The nose-twitching, head-quivering were to her mind movements of refinement, signaling appreciation.

He looked at her, triumphant. Just as he'd said all along. Neither would ever find another so perfectly suited. This was why he wanted to buy an island in Tigre and make it her kingdom.

"What will you call the island in Tigre?" It suddenly occurred to me to ask.

How I liked their grandiose, elaborate imaginations. How bored I was with false, Protestant humility, a whole race stifled, cramped, craving attention but unable to solicit it, waiting for someone to come along and marvel over what they were hiding away. Yes, marvel at yourself, I thought, looking at them, that's the way to live. Don't wait for some other wretch to do it. And here in this moment I appreciated the idea of the island.

Still, I didn't entirely understand what he was doing here. He wasn't stupid. In his eyes was a wild look. He must have seen it himself in the mirror. He hadn't ever met anyone like her. His ex-wife had been the opposite, a steady, tranquil person. This girl was playing with him. And he let himself be played with.

Looking more closely, I could also see that he was tired, a tired player. He had nothing like Leonarda's stamina, ambition. His sense of enjoyment was different. Was it maybe even more intense, sweeter than ours? He was nearing fifty. Was this his last opportunity for something?

We moved to the living room. I asked him if he ever smoked all those pipes that were lying on his desk. Twisting, bowing—his physical demeanor certainly was strange—he said he did occasionally. I asked if he'd please smoke one now, I wanted to see him.

"Oh, yes, Daddy, smoke one," she said, child-like, as if it would be a big childish treat for us all.

The living room looked in on the bedroom. I remembered earlier scenes on that bed, Leonarda there, offering me her voluptuous breasts. The apartment was inhabited by these ghost scenes, her coming out of the bathroom with a mustache on, kissing me in the hallway. Suddenly, I felt irritated all over again, thinking how those scenes must be mixed in her mind with similar scenes she'd lived here with him.

Miguel lit a pipe, embarrassed, delighted, exposing himself. Could the guy stop for a moment exposing himself? Angry, I looked away. This is going to be interminable, I thought, suddenly depressed, and I sat down on the couch. Leonarda sat with me. She was all wiggly, squirmy. At the touch of her squirminess, I felt squirmy too, despite myself. He was standing by his desk, smoking, watching us. He turned his neck, stretching, and an enormous tendon stood out.

"Ohhhhh, look at that!" Leonarda said. "Do that again."

He did it again. Once again I was picking up on her giddiness, getting lost inside the evil of the moment, its playfulness. It was also the touch of her squirmy legs. We were under the operating-table lamp. Her breast was pressed against my arm. I could feel the stiff nipple.

"Oh, wait," she said, getting up on her knees, leaning over me, her large full breasts against my shoulder, then neck, then cheek, then the top of my head. I turned my mouth to suck them. She was adjusting the lamp, so it was more directly on us. "There," she said, but without coming down from her knees. Now her breasts were near my face. She pressed them into my face, looking over her shoulder at him.

"She likes to suck my breasts," she said, "you should see how she sucks them."

I made a sound. I had my eyes shut now. I tried to get her nipple in my mouth.

"See, I told you, she gets so excited," she said. "I don't let her suck them at first and then I do."

She was moving her breasts around in front of my face, not letting me latch on. I grabbed one and bit the nipple through the shirt—she cried out—then sucked.

"Oh," she said, "see, I can't stop her."

She was wearing the striped T-shirt of a boy. She lifted it. I pulled at her bra. Eyes still closed, I wanted her breast in my mouth. I pushed the bra up so the breast spilled out.

"See," she said, "you're not the only one who desires me."

I wanted to devour her breast, take the whole thing in my mouth.

"See now, wouldn't you like to be fucking me right now?" she said.

He must have started to move.

"Don't move!" she said. "Stay right there, just take off your pants. I want to see your ugly horn sticking out." He, staying over by the desk, slowly removed his pants.

She touched my hair. "You know what she likes? She likes it in the ass. I told you about her splendid ass. If you do what we say, she'll offer it up to you."

I made a sound of protest.

"Don't worry, she'll do it, if I let her keep sucking. She does whatever I say. You know what I pictured? After this, what I picture? You know the ham on the spit in the kitchen? I pictured the two of us putting you under this lamp, and cutting you up like a pig on a spit—"

I saw the image very clearly, him cored on a spit, his long lower limbs dangling off. Suddenly, the whole thing seemed horrible to me. I jerked my head away from Leonarda's breast, pushed her off of me.

"That's it, I'm going," I said.

Finding my way to the door, I glanced back once as I closed it. He was standing, pants down, rabbit teeth showing. Leonarda was still up on her knees on the couch. Moments later, I was on the street walking fast past the zoo, the animals breathing on the other side of the wall. Leonarda called me but I didn't answer. Later, I checked the message: "Hey, why did you leave?" it said.

nineteen

There was a puddle of water outside my door when I got home. This was not entirely unusual because part of the wall was open to the sky, so sometimes it would rain or leaves would fall in onto the floor. But this puddle extended underneath the door. I opened the door and indeed it was part of a much larger puddle, more like a long shallow pool, that extended all the way down the black-and-white-checkered hall. At the end, where the kitchen was, I saw a glimmering mass, deeper water still. I hurried to the source, not without a quick peek on the way into the living room. The rug was submerged in about an inch of water. My sneakers were soon soaked, but that was the least of my problems. I got to the kitchen, where water was steadily pouring out from the little white cabinet beneath the sink. I opened the cabinet. Water gurgled copiously from one of the pipes. I knelt down and put my hands around the pipe. There was so much pressure, the water shot through my fingers, the gurgling curves turned into violent spray. I stood up and peered into the living room again. The lower legs of the furniture were all submerged.

I called Olga and left a message on her cell phone. I opened the front door and peered out into the hall. Could somebody help me? As usual, there was no one around. I climbed one flight up where I'd once seen a man with dark hair in an overcoat enter his apartment and turn on a Mahler symphony. I knocked on the door. No one. Then it occurred to me that the more urgent scenario was the one downstairs. Those were the people who would be suffering my leak. I went down to the apartment below and knocked. I did hear sounds, but it took a moment for someone to appear. Finally, a young man with silky dark hair and blunt features opened the door.

"What is it?" he asked.

"I live upstairs. My apartment's flooding. I was afraid the water might be coming down here too."

"I haven't noticed anything," he said.

"Do you own the place?"

"No, no, I don't. I just work here. I'm with a client now."

As he was talking, I saw a darkening patch of water on the wall behind him. "There, there it is!" I said.

He turned and looked. "Oh, yeah."

But he didn't seem that concerned. Or rather, he seemed much more concerned with what he was doing.

"Hey," a voice called out behind him.

"I'll just finish up something and then I'll call the owner. Thank you, thank you very much." And he closed the door in my face.

Of course, he's doing Gabriel's job, I thought. I called Gabriel and left a message, describing the situation and asking him to call me back.

I returned to the leaking pipe in my kitchen. Wasn't there caulk or something I could put on it? Tape, Super Glue? I looked in the cupboards and various drawers of the furniture. Nothing.

Meanwhile, the water was rising on the floor. I could monitor the water level by looking at the far wall of the living room. Nearby were doors that opened onto the balcony. The least I could do, I thought, is open those doors. I crossed and opened them. Water flushed out onto the balcony and fell in a sheet down into the back garden. The day was the same as it had been earlier, calm and rosy. Looking down, I saw someone in the garden. Could this be the reclusive super? This man who I felt sure existed, but was impossible to find. When I'd asked Olga about him, she too had seemed vague. "There is a super," she'd said, "or there was. I've never seen him myself."

"Hey," I yelled. "Help!" By now I was just shouting at the receding back of a man, the top of his head, slightly balding, strong, rounded shoulders. Without even a glance, he stepped back inside.

I turned back to the room. The whole situation felt out of my hands. I was in a foreign city, in a place not my own, no one was helping me. I pictured the water steadily rising, inch by inch, as high as a foot. Soon I'd be wading through the rooms, like people waded across the streets when it flooded here, the water at my shins, then knees, then thighs. At some point, I'd have to simply get the hell out of here. I'd pack my things and walk out with my bag, leaving the apartment, the whole building, to rot and crumble. What else was I supposed to do?

But I wasn't ready to abandon ship yet. Staring at the semi-submerged room, I decided that one thing I could do was go around and pick up everything possible and put it on higher ground, while I waited for either Olga or Gabriel to call. I picked up all my possessions, shoes and bags and clothes, and then the apartment owner's possessions, where possible. I cleared the books out of the lower shelves of the bookcases and put them on the table. I put smaller furniture on top of unmovable items. But wait, wouldn't the best thing be to turn the water off entirely? I thought of the last time when I'd had no water, the whole situation of the water tank and valves on the roof. Remembering the details of this kind of thing was not my forté, but at least I could go up there and give it a shot.

As I was walking up the stairs, Gabriel called. My description of what was happening came out nonsensically.

"Okay, okay," he said. "I'll call Hugo. And I'll come by myself too, as soon as I can."

I went up on the roof. I looked at the tank, the valves. As far as I could see, there were two possible valves, or valve-like appendages. I turned one of them, turned it back, then turned it again. The only way to know would be if I went back downstairs again. I went back downstairs. The water was still streaming out of the pipe. I could only imagine what was happening below. I pictured that dark swath of water I'd already seen. Now that whole wall must be dark and wet.

The person I should really be calling is the owner of the apartment, or rather the owner's brother. This had occurred to me before and I had asked Olga for his number, but she'd said he didn't want to be involved with the tenants. Everything had to go through her.

As I stepped out my door to go up to the roof again, I heard music coming from the apartment upstairs. Had the guy just come home? I went upstairs again and rang his bell. Again, no answer. This guy clearly didn't want to be disturbed. I could respect that. Still, this was a particular situation. I continued up onto the roof, where I climbed up to the water tank again and turned the second valve.

I was carrying my cell phone with me everywhere. Right after I turned the valve, Olga called. She sounded distressed. I felt like telling her I was much more distressed. She was out in Olivos, a wealthy suburb, where she was showing houses to a client who was looking for a swimming pool. She'd call the brother. She'd try to be there as soon as she could.

When I got back downstairs, I noticed a silence. Or at least a new kind of sound, gentle lapping. The water had ceased pouring out. I checked to be sure. Yes, it really had stopped. The pipe below the sink stood there gleaming uneventfully.

I got a broom and started sweeping the water out onto the balcony. It sloshed down into the back garden. I did this for a while and then Gabriel showed up. There was still an inch or so of water on the floor.

"Christ, dude! What's wrong with this apartment?" he said.

"At least I managed to turn the water off," I said. "You should have seen it before."

He followed me into the living room and looked around. "Shit, girl, this is not a good scene."

"I feel like we should get as much water out as we can," I said. "So things don't rot."

"Okay, let's do it. Hugo's on his way."

I handed Gabriel the broom and told him to sweep the water

off the balcony with that. I went and got the mop and all the towels I had. He swept and I mopped. Then we both got down on the floor and soaked up all the water we could in the towels, wringing them out over the balcony at intervals and coming back for more. By the end, we were both sweating and tired. We lay there, he on the chaise lounge, me on a chair, exhausted.

Olga called again, sounding frazzled. I said the plumber was arriving. "Oh, good," she said. She was still out in Olivos. Her client was "very demanding." She whispered this into the phone.

Gabriel sent Hugo another text. He was on another job, would be there as soon as possible.

"So how's everything?" Gabriel asked.

I told him about the latest scene with Leonarda and Miguel.

"I remember once when I didn't know what to do, I went away to this place in Uruguay," he said. "It's, like, this little squatters' settlement on the beach. You can't get there by car. You have to walk over the dunes. Or you can pay for a jeep to take you. There's no electricity or running water. I went there because someone had told me about it. I was alone, I wasn't sure what to do next, and when I was there I had this sort of panic attack. Yeah, way out there, in the middle of fucking nowhere. That was an important point in my life."

"And then what? What happened?"

"I came back and started studying to be a doctor. Yeah, really."

Once he'd left, I felt agitated. I got up and wandered around the apartment. I looked in the mirror. The more I stared, the weirder my face appeared. For the hundredth time, I looked through the owner's things, the books, knickknacks, tape cassettes. I pulled out a book, a novel, whose spine said *La Creciente*. I looked up *creciente* in my English–Spanish dictionary. It meant "tide." I sat down and read the opening:

The city was constructed on the edge of a river, but it wasn't a companionable river on whose shores inhabitants could walk, that linked up between welcoming piers, under bridges with memorable names, one of those rivers that it was enough to mention to situate immediately the city which is its near-synonym: the Seine, the Tiber, the Thames, the Guadalquivir, the Moscow. It was a river independent from the city like a watery slice attached to it, a river that men didn't need to cross to go from one end of the city to another, that did not impose itself on their vision and about which they hardly ever thought, since weeks and even months could pass without seeing it. They only went to it in the summer, but for this it was necessary to go a good distance from the city.

It was a South American city and maybe for this reason the river was different from those of European cities. Everything about South America is different from Europe, something that saddens and humiliates the inhabitants of this continent, even leading them to deny this reality. Its landscapes, its people, its elements, its political events, its rivers are different. It was difficult to reach this particular river. A foreigner, attracted one day by the copper color of its waters, scenes on a postcard, wanted to find it and throw in a coin, an indispensable ritual when you arrive at any city where there's a river. He was a determined and meticulous man, since Nordic blood ran in his veins and no one can deny that Nordic people know how to plan their days and accomplish their plans. He went down to the big avenues that run along the river and then turned on a transversal street. It was closed. He repeated his attempts tirelessly over the course of the day. At one point he encountered a wall that was hundreds of meters long. When he arrived at the end of it, he thought he saw the river, but it was only a barrier; he went to the other end of the street entrance and saw a sign that said "Closed to traffic." His patience and perseverance did not flag, he had been a boy scout from the age of seven and a mountain climber since he was eleven; he had waited an entire year in the Siegfried Line and two and a half in a concentration camp, so he could definitely dedicate a day to looking for the river. But night fell and he still hadn't found the way.

The following morning, he repeated his search, he ran into other walls, other barriers, other streets closed to traffic, long rows of warehouses, coast guards who prevented his passing, rusted rails with out-of-use wagons put there like barricades and always, at the end, as if making fun of him, the tall masts that proclaimed the existence of the river. I don't know how this apparently fruitless persecution ended, and it isn't especially related to this story in any case apart from the definite fact that people had forgotten that they had a river and they neither feared nor enjoyed it. Maybe the foreigner managed to make it out from the top of a modern building or possibly he had to travel several kilometers away in order finally to catch a glimpse of the river on whose shores the city had been constructed.

I called Gabriel. "Hey, what's the name of that place in Uruguay? I think you're right, I need to go away and think."

Part III

twenty

It took pretty much a whole day to get there. I took a midnight ferry across the Río de la Plata, the brown water transformed by night and the movement of the boat into a black sheet scattered continuously with white diamonds. We arrived at three in the morning in the port of Colonia. Then a six-hour bus drive across Uruguay into the dawn. It was a small country—I'd looked it up—roughly the size of my home state, Washington.

I was sitting in the very front of the bus and watched the sun come up through the slanted windshield. The landscape was soft and green, with reddish roads, stands of eucalyptus, comforting clumps of sheep. Just looking out at it made me feel quieter. I had my iPod on and drifted in and out of sleep. Finally, we pulled in at an outpost where there were several jeeps parked around a wooden ticket booth. After I waited for an hour or so, a jeep took me and a few other passengers across the dunes to the fishing village that was my destination.

I was glad to get away, to have my mind filled with new impressions. I made a point of not thinking about the things I'd come away to think about, at least not at first. I wanted to flood my mind with this other world, so that by the time I did think of them, it would be a different mind thinking.

As Gabriel had said, there was no running water or electricity here. I had a little wooden cabin set back from the beach, a bucket, a well. During the day, I wandered down to the beach. The sand was packed hard. The waves were long. At certain points, they looked especially turbulent, as if currents were meeting, and could suck you right down. There were people here and there, not many. I walked along. A woman was selling crushed whale bones in little vials, which she claimed were aphrodisiacs. In the distance were high dunes, scaling, plunging. Every now and then, a dark tiny figure appeared on top of one of them, looked out, paused and then started to descend, stick-like legs sinking deep into the sand. There were dolphins in the water. Farther along were seal carcasses washed up on the shore, sometimes just the bones, sometimes the whole body, giving off a putrid smell.

Back in my cabin, I lay down on the floor. Sometimes when I lay there, I felt a sensation in my chest, a sort of pressing feeling. It was oddly soothing, as if there were a hand resting there. Occasionally, I could summon the feeling, usually not. But if the feeling was there and I kept my awareness on the spot, the sensation grew. Sometimes it hurt. Sometimes it felt nice.

The days melted into one another. I began waking up much earlier than I ever would. In the early mornings, the sky was a deep crazy pink. I thought about things I wouldn't have thought about otherwise, the way the water curves down the drain in one direction in the northern hemisphere and in another in the south. Consequently, rivers also carve different paths, the high bank on one side in the north, on the other in the south.

I noticed the way the long grasses, swirling in the wind, left their own form of hieroglyphics, grass writing, circles in the sand. I stared down at the imprints left by tidal streams, those wavy patterns, like the form of the branches of trees, the shape of neurons, blood vessels, the shape of everything. From a certain spot on the dunes, you could see the sun and moon at the same time. I remembered things I had learned years ago. Sand actually consists of sea shells crushed tiny. Tides are the moon pulling water toward itself. To this day, no one understands why.

It's true that sometimes when staring at a tidal imprint in the sand, Leonarda in her various incarnations would come into my mind. At times I felt revulsion, especially when thinking of that last scene. Why get involved with such people who treated each other cruelly, wished each other harm? Then I'd see her in a different light, how fragile she was, the confessions she'd made to me. Another day, I had a vision of birds on branches hung with blossoms, moving in the wind. The birds took off, landed again, took off, this light, bright happiness I had felt with her. I thought of how it was in the beginning, just the two of us playing out in the world, before she'd introduced the Master Plan. What I wanted was to return to that early state, if we possibly could.

A general retreats from battle, hunkers down in the hills. I had come away to nurse my wounds, recuperate and think through my next move. I would use all the tricks I had at my disposal. She could change shapes all she wanted. I didn't care. Underneath was something else, I felt sure of it, this warm furry creature, sitting there quietly, waiting for me.

I stayed away a month. But even on returning to Buenos Aires, I didn't call Leonarda right away. I wanted to be careful, to do this right. The city had emptied out in my absence, as I'd been told it always did at this time of year. Isolde was in Uruguay, a different part than where I had been, Punta del Este, where the summer parties were. I called the hairdresser's to make an appointment with Vera, but she was also at the beach, the Argentine coast. And Leonarda? For a moment, I imagined that she'd gone away with him, that the two of them were in Tigre, swanning along the muddy waterways, checking out island properties together. I panicked for a moment, was about to call her, then lay down on the floor for as long as I needed to, to calm myself down.

The city was too hot for comfort. The streets were glaring.

I saw Gabriel. He'd had to stay in town for his messenger work. He seemed languid from the heat. But he approved of my taking time to think things through. I could tell that he approved.

The botanist had gotten in touch. He was very excited about a story happening on Argentine soil, a flower, the *Iris pseudacorus* that was taking over the Argentine wetlands. This was typical of him. He'd get very excited about a particular plant case and follow it closely.

"Have you heard about it?" he asked.

I hadn't, but I promised to keep my ears open.

I turned again to my water research. I had less than three months to go before I sent in my final report. I spent a number of afternoons in the National Public Library doing research. I took a tour of the water purification plant, witnessing how the dirty water from the Río de la Plata got transformed into the clear liquid that found its way into buildings and houses.

Finally, after three weeks of this, I called.

twenty-one

Heyyyyy, hiiiiiiiiiiiii!" Leonarda said. "You have no idea how much you want to see me."

I picked her up after her Chinese lesson.

She was wearing a tiny miniskirt, sneakers and her glasses. "Oh, wait, we have to put on makeup." We stopped under a streetlight. It was dusk again. A dog was lying in the open door of a garage. "You need green, I always told you," she said. "Close your eyes." She put deep shimmering green shadow on my eyelids.

We came to a plaza, its pathways on diagonals, the trees enormous, benches minuscule. All that green in the darkness, hulked there, breathing.

I was trying to keep my equanimity. One part of my brain, a stronghold, wouldn't budge. But another part was buckling, even now, I could feel it. Okay, go ahead, colonize.

The point was I needed to stay in charge. Seduce, enchant, those things too, but above all take control of how the evening would unfold.

She looked over at me with a funny smile. "You're grateful to us, aren't you?" she said. "Our antics free you up."

I raised my eyebrows. I didn't mind what I assumed to be her jealousy, her fear of losing full dominion over me.

"You're that kind of foreigner. You go somewhere exotic and start moving your butt"—she circled her little butt around; some guys hooted from their cars—"and suddenly you think you've had an epiphany, like you've understood everything about yourself and the world."

I laughed. Oh, yeah, the butt fixation. I'd forgotten about that.

"Or at least your butt's understood. The knowledge is collected in your butt, which, by the way"—she glanced back—"is getting bigger and bigger."

We walked on. The enchantment accumulated. Despite my wariness, stronger than me. I imagined zoo animals in wartime, having crept out of their bomb-shattered cages, wandering loose on the streets.

Suddenly, we were bumped into from behind. Leonarda skittered to one side. I fell forward, catching myself with one hand.

"Hey!" she yelled. "What the fuck?"

It was one of the *cartoneros,* the people who collect recyclable garbage. He was pushing a canvas cart suspended on wheels in which to amass his loot. It was piled taller than he was, blocking his view.

Leonarda walked around the side of the cart. "Dude, you knocked us over! What's the deal?"

"Sorry, I'm really sorry." The guy, surprised to be addressed at all by someone like her, and especially so informally, was about her age. He did look sorry.

"Well, whatever. Get it together," Leonarda said, turning away. "C'mon, dufus," she called to me.

I crossed the street to where she was.

"I know," she said, grabbing my hand in her little, hot one. "Let's go to the nerd bar. It's right near here."

By "nerds," she meant hackers, computer program designers, video game inventors, maybe the kind of people she most admired, because they were at the forefront of everything.

"You know Mercury fell apart," she told me on the way. "I knew it would. It was totally passé. This is the new center of operations. Welcome to nerd world!"

The bar was dark, everything looked red, with black-and-white cow spots here and there. Leonarda hoisted herself onto a barstool and sat there, shoulders hunched.

When the bartender came, she ordered a beer. I got one too.

There was a very tall guy with a very short woman at the end of the bar.

"Shit," Leonarda said, "sexual vertigo."

Suddenly, her face lit up. "Ohhh, the skydiver!"

A young man with dark hair was sitting about five stools down from us. He seemed to have been waiting for her to recognize him. He got up, beer in hand, and came over.

Leonarda turned to me. "This is Mateo. He's a skydiver and a nerd. It's the best combination."

"Oh, wow," I said. "I'd like to try the skydiving part."

"If you're serious, I can arrange it," the guy said. "The one thing I would say is that you should do it more than once. You have to do it a few times to really enjoy it."

"Like how many times?" I asked.

He shrugged. "After the fiftieth jump you begin to enjoy it."

"Fiftieth jump? Jesus."

"I would never do that," Leonarda said, scowling.

"Why?" Mateo asked.

"Because I make a point of living my life so I don't take risks."

"You do?" I asked, surprised.

"But you cross the street?" Mateo said.

"I cross the street in a way that it's one hundred percent sure that it's not a risk."

Mateo and I laughed.

"How did you two meet?" he asked.

"I stalked her," Leonarda said.

"You did?"

"Yeah, I began stalking her online. I found out where she lived and waited outside on the pavement. I followed her everywhere." Her eyes had an eerie look, making her story sound totally believable.

A further group of nerds entered.

"I know that guy," Leonarda said, pointing to one of them, her lips close against my ear. "From the university. He's a famous hacker. Like, I mean, he hacked through the U.S. Department of State's security system."

The guy seemed to recognize her too, but was shy. Mateo went over to talk to the group.

"So anyway, where were we?" she said, turning back to me. "Oh, yeah, you as a product of Humboldt's theory."

We were like a comedy sketch. I lifted my eyebrows, meaning "Who's Humboldt?" She rolled her eyes, meaning "Moron."

"Humboldt, you know, the Austrian explorer naturalist," she said. "Bolívar, like the friggin' liberator of the continent, called Humboldt the true discoverer of America. He traveled around here for, like, five years, doing all kinds of tests, describing everything, from ocean currents to volcanoes to magnetic fields to plant life. It's not exactly that he came up with original ideas" (at this, I smiled—I knew how much she prized the "original idea") "but he had, like, an astonishing capacity to synthesize knowledge. One of his essays called 'The Geography of Plants' is about how the geographic environment influences plant life, in which he pretty much laid down the foundations for ecology."

I nodded. I felt extremely happy to be sitting here in the nerd bar, listening to Leonarda talk about Humboldt, the nerds in the background, the couple with sexual vertigo at the far end of the bar.

"So I was saying that obviously this geographical location is having its effects on you. Really, I think it's great how you're interacting with your environment."

She stopped for a second and stared. She looked sad. And then suddenly she was crying.

"What? What is it?" I asked.

"No, forget it. You didn't want to see me."

She had taken off her glasses. "My face looks wrong without the glasses, doesn't it?"

"It looks beautiful," I said. "The glasses are protection."

"Yeah, you're right"—putting them back on—"the glasses are protection."

The night was getting away from me. It acquired a slant. Next we were dancing, then climbing across the red-and-black furniture, chasing each other. She made a wrong turn. I caught and kissed her.

The night cracked open further. We were in a car, speeding along dark roads outside the city. The star hacker who had broken into the U.S. security system was driving. Two other nerds were with us. We stopped, stepped out.

"Where are we?" I asked.

"By the river," Leonarda said.

"I don't see it."

"It's over there." Leonarda pointed ahead. We were walking across a plain lit by tall lamps that gave off a greenish glow.

"It's like a sports field," I said.

The air was full of moisture, soft and white. I looked over and saw the star hacker and his friends at a slight distance advancing in tandem. They looked ghostly, otherworldly, as if enveloped in a haze of light. Ahead was darkness, where the river was supposed to be. The river, I would finally reach it, stand on its shore, put my toes in that water. But instead of a shore, we arrived at a barrier of black, asteroid-shaped chunks of debris.

"What's this?" I asked.

We stepped up onto the debris. There was a wall of it that toppled down as far as the water.

"This is so the river won't devour us," Leonarda said.

I looked down the coast. The massive debris was sprinkled along it as far as the eye could see.

"If this weren't here, that whole field behind us would be deep in water," Leonarda continued. "And not only that, but water would be creeping down those streets beyond it, filling all the alleys and basements, rising slowly to higher ground."

I looked at her. I drank in the old enchantment, yet with a grain of salt.

Next we were alone, in a trucker joint, eating chorizos. Leonarda was starving.

"Your nails look nice," I said. They were bright orange-red against the chorizo sandwich.

"Yeah, my mother did them." Her mother, the glowering monster?

We were in a cab, going back to my house, passing the zoo. She leaned forward to talk to the driver. "Can we stop here for a second?"

The taxi pulled over. We were in front of Miguel's house.

"Why?" I said. "What are you doing?"

"There's a book I need. It'll be quick."

"Wait." I looked at her intently. "If you're not ready to go home, we can do something else. We can go dancing."

She shrugged. "Yeah, sure. But let's go in here for a sec."

This was the moment to keep my head. "I'm not interested," I said, not budging from the taxi seat.

Leonarda sighed with exasperation, reached over and grabbed my hand. I resisted, feeling at the same time that everything was slipping out of my grasp again.

"Hey, girls, what's going on?" the taxi driver said.

"Nothing," she answered, then turned to me. "I have to go in for two minutes. I swear, it's important."

We rang the bell. It was late, like three in the morning. He was awake. Or rather, it seemed he had been dozing, but was still fully dressed. He didn't seem that surprised to see us.

We stepped inside. It was strange. Leonarda's pink jersey mini-dress was bunched up on the couch under the hospital light. Then I saw what looked like her computer. She loved her computer like a human being, never left it anywhere, slept with it by her bed at night. I looked at her.

But she had turned away, down the hall. Still groggy, Miguel had lit a pipe, was standing by his desk. I followed Leonarda.

"This apartment's fine," she said, "but the bathroom's horrible, small and dingy. I've told him it's horrible. He has to fix it."

She turned off into the little room where his son slept when he stayed there. I followed. The last thing I wanted was to be left alone with him. More of Leonarda's things were here. The bed was unmade. Her notebooks were spread around amid the rumpled sheets.

"What the fuck?" I whispered. "Are you staying here?"

"Shh," she said, whispering back. "No, I was just sick. And my mother was so horrible. She threw me out."

"And so you came here?"

"I had nowhere else to go."

I was looking down at the little bed, at her notebooks full of small crabbed writing, impossible to decipher though I'd tried more than once. Too dumbfounded to think, I sat down on the bed. "I can't believe this."

She went and closed the door. Oh, that's right, I thought, to make matters worse, there was that horrible creature out there listening.

"Have you forgotten the Master Plan?" she asked.

"The Master Fucking Plan says you're supposed to live with him?"

"I'm not living with him. I'm just staying for a few days in the kid's room. How do you think they poisoned Roman emperors? Someone has to be on the inside. I told him you were my girlfriend and that would never change."

I laughed an awful-tasting laugh. This girlfriend thing was new too.

But she was enthusiastic. "Listen, it's really working." By now, she'd sat down beside me and was whispering heatedly into my ear. "He's getting more and more dependent on my mind. It's like he can't think without me. He can't even write his shitty little articles without asking me first what I think." She laughed. Then a second later withdrew her lips from my ear. She was suddenly wan-faced, staring off into the corner of the room. "If things go on like this, it'll soon be over."

"Why?" I asked, clinging despite myself to this glimmer of hope.

"Well, obviously, it'll get too boring. It almost already is."

That was it. If that was her only concern . . . "Okay, I have to go," I said, standing abruptly.

"Wait, what is wrong with you? Stay for a drink at least."

"A drink?" I looked at her, my face disgusted. But the truth was I felt trapped. If I walked out of this room, I'd have to pass by him, exit defeated. This was more than I could bear. My eye lit on the little window. I could climb out there into the garden.

"Wait, I know," she said. "Why don't you stay the night? Oh, please.

Stay here with me. It'll be so adorable. We'll sleep together in this little bed." She curled up on the bed and rubbed her upper arm with her hand. "My skin's just getting softer and softer, like a nymphet's."

I ignored her and walked over to the window. It was small, like everything else in the room.

She sat up. "What are you doing, dufus?"

I pulled the window up.

She leaped off the bed, pointing at me and whispering furiously. "I'll be so ashamed if you act jealous. That gives him power, don't you see? Then he has power over us."

"Whatever, Leonarda, this is your fucking gig. It has nothing to do with me."

"What are you saying? You don't understand anything." But I wasn't even looking at her. I was facing the window, starting to climb out.

"Your butt's never going to fit through there," she said.

But it did. I was outside now.

"You're really stupid, you know that. Much, much stupider than I thought." But I was already walking away.

I crossed the dark garden to the door that led into the lobby, opened it and started across the lobby.

"Wait." I heard her voice, breathless, behind me. She had rushed through the apartment and come out into the hall. "What do you want?"

I turned and looked at her. "I want you to come with me," I said.

She fell silent, like a child, wanting to obey. "Okay," she said.

She went back into the apartment and reappeared a few minutes later, a little backpack stuffed with her things, computer, notebooks, pink jersey dress.

She followed me out the front door of the building. I was standing on the street, hailing a cab.

"Hey," she said.

I looked at her. "What?" I asked.

She squirmed, smiled. It was a sweet, wary smile. "I'm sorry," she said. "I'm not very good in those adult situations," and turned back and went inside.

Okay, that was that. I went back to my apartment. I stayed there for a few days, mostly lying in bed, blinds closed, defeat. Every once in a while, my cell phone rang. I didn't answer it. Even when it was Leonarda. I had come that far. All I knew was that I was in a trap, from which I needed to extricate myself. I had no other clear thoughts but that one. I lay there in the trap. The pain was pretty much constant, no matter which way I turned. Sometimes when I twisted, provoked by a certain image or thought—the two of them waking up together, having breakfast; working together, she liked to sit in bed, knees up, with her computer, he'd be at his desk; then darkness outside the window, evening falling, sexy scenes, her playing her transformation games with him—the pain cut more sharply, yanking ligaments, tearing fur and skin. But there were ancillary thoughts too. What did I really want? For the darkness to have that same freshness, the air to shimmer, as it did when

I was with her. There was also something I knew I didn't want, for her to be with that guy. I shivered just thinking of him touching her skin. Then I'd shake myself and return to the point. How to get out of this? Go away again? Return home? What was there for me? I couldn't picture anything. Except maybe the hospital. Illness awaited.

Days went by. I ate all the meager amount of food that was in the house, including cooking the rice and pasta that had been left by someone else. I looked in the mirror a lot. I looked like an undecided creature, definitely part animal. Oh, why couldn't I let myself just be an animal? That was fine. It was the other part that was causing problems. I remembered what Gabriel had once said about desire, that horrible yearning.

One day, I heard her out in the hall. Then I remembered. She had keys. I'd once given her an extra set of keys. I heard her block heels, her harsh, hulking gait. I remembered what I'd once learned about espionage. You can change your face entirely, get plastic surgery. The one thing that's almost impossible to change is the way you walk. In counterespionage, always look for the walk. I rushed to the door, put the safe-lock across it, then crept back down the tiled hall. Sitting on my bed again, I heard the key in the door. It opened and then the safe-lock jerked it back.

"I know you're in there," she said. "I hear you breathing."

I stopped breathing. I didn't move. For some reason, I felt wildly afraid.

"Come out, little reptile, that's right, little snake."

I still didn't answer.

"Okay, whatever, open the door." Now her voice was tired, bored. I was amazed at myself that I still wasn't moving.

"I'm bored."

Silence.

"You know, you're really an idiot. You misunderstood everything. I can't do this without you."

Silence.

"Anyway, I'm back at my mother's place."

Here she knew she could get me. She almost did. I felt myself rise from the mattress, but no.

Next there was banging. She was banging the door against the safe-lock.

Silence again.

"Anyway, whatever. I really can't waste my time with such stupid people." I heard her heels again, this time receding.

I felt a little better. At least she'd come for me. But that didn't change things in any essential way. I was still trapped and still needed to extricate myself and still didn't know how.

I called Gabriel. He stopped by later that afternoon.

"Hey, what's going on? What are you doing here?" He looked at me more closely. "Jesus, what happened?"

I told him.

"Oh, that's bad. Let me just check something. You look very pale." He checked my pulse, my glands, my tongue, my eyeballs. When he was finished, he sat back. "It seems like you're all right, but you have to get out of here, get up, move around. What about your water project? You should do some research or write it up or something. Okay, listen, I've got a client downstairs. I'll pick you up as soon as I'm done."

"So what are you going to do?" Gabriel asked once he'd come back upstairs and found me in nearly the exact same position.

"I don't know." I felt weak.

"You know what? I think you should get some other sex in your life."

"Oh," I said. It was really the last thing on my mind. I felt so weak.

"You know 'eros' is life, they say."

"Mmm, maybe."

"C'mon, I'll go with you."

I pointed at myself. "Now?"

"Sure. Why not?"

He took me to a little bar on a corner. It looked familiar. Then I remembered, I'd been here at the beginning with Leonarda. We went downstairs and ordered whiskies. There were a few people, not many, milling around. It was way early for Buenos Aires. The place was like a firetrap for sure, dark with no exits. Cell phones here and there illuminated people's faces. Gabriel by this light looked very delicate, his skin pink and gold.

The whiskey warmed me up in a great way. A song came on and Gabriel and I went out onto the dance floor. There was no one else dancing. We danced theatrically, interpreting the songs. I had never really danced that way with anyone. At one point, I looked up, peering into his face. Could we be in love?

We sat down again at the bar. A young man was checking Gabriel out.

"Anyone you like?" Gabriel asked, looking around.

I hadn't been in this situation for so long, since before my marriage really.

"I think you should turn," Gabriel said. "Yeah, that's right, rotate, no, to your left. There's a guy there who's looking at you."

I turned slightly, glanced.

"You have to turn a little more," Gabriel said.

"I'm not sure I can do this right now," I said.

"Of course you can. I'm going to look away. I don't want him to think you're with me. Smile. Say hi. Or just smile, that's enough. When you do talk, show some accent. People like that. Sexy and helpless. Exotic, whatever."

I did turn and did smile.

"Hi," the guy said. "Do you want to dance?"

We danced. This was okay, it felt easier than talking anyway. At one point, we even danced close and I could feel his dick clearly in his pants.

We danced a few more songs. Gabriel was now talking to the guy who'd been watching him.

A little bit later, my guy asked, "You want to come home with me?"

I shrugged. I guess that had been the plan, right? "Okay," I said.

I went and told Gabriel and got my things.

In the taxi, I felt completely baffled that I was going home with this guy. Is this really what people do? I didn't say anything.

Happily, when we got to his place, the guy, whose name was Pablo, had some pot. This changed things. After taking a few puffs, I felt that I was shimmering, flowing, and everything around me was shimmering and flowing too. I leaned forward to sip my drink.

Rather than a repulsive creature worthy of scorn or a possible menace, the guy I was with seemed like a warm animal body sharing this room with me, someone who, if need be, I could cuddle up to.

It's surprising how little, in these circumstances, people wish each other harm.

I did move over toward him and cuddled in his armpit. He put his hand down and caressed my hair. This is what people do, I thought. They meet and within an hour or two are cuddling into each other's armpits, stroking each other's hair.

twenty-two

Isolde had left me lots of messages to which, in my fugue state, I hadn't replied. Now I called her back. We met. She was ebullient. She had found a job. She told me all about it.

The organization, run by a woman named Alicia, auctioned off art and gave the proceeds to charity groups for children. Perfect, everything Isolde was interested in. She'd begun working a week ago. They were long days. Isolde got up early in the mornings and went to Alicia's office, which was in the front part of her full-floor apartment. From that moment until the end of the day, she did everything Alicia bid her.

Alicia dressed in beautiful, colorful clothes. On her travels around the various South American capitals, she always went to look at new designers' collections. She'd come back with long patch-work evening dresses, necklaces made of cloth. She'd had some plastic surgery done, but tastefully, tastefully. She only went to the best doctors, the ones that foreigners used—Argentina has long been a destination, along with Brazil, for plastic surgery candidates from around the world. You can get quality work done for a very decent price. Among another class of foreigners of lesser means, it's also a place to do complex dentistry. The families of middle-class Americans who visit them here always schedule to get their dental work done at the same time, root canals, caps. An added benefit, along with price, is that foreigners can spend a few weeks incognito, only returning to their version of civilization once their wounds have healed.

Isolde brought Alicia tea when the maid had stepped out. She made unimportant calls. Her accent worked in her favor. She looked at children's charities on the Internet, marking ones that looked promising. She had hoped to get more involved in the art angle. Had she been too pushy here? Alicia seemed to like to deal with that side herself.

The difficulty was that Alicia was absentminded. She'd forget to tell Isolde to do something and then get angry when it wasn't done. She was terribly disorganized. She'd go to a meeting and forget her notes. But she had power, she had money, she was seductive and able to win people over. In Alicia's absentmindedness, Isolde saw her niche. She could help Alicia to structure her life. She began prompting Alicia to call that person or write that letter.

"This is where I feel like I can really help her," Isolde told me. "I can make her whole life smoother in a way she can't imagine. Soon, I'll become indispensable to her."

After our lunch, Isolde went back to the office. It was Monday, Alicia was in San Pablo, returning that afternoon in time for a board meeting in her office. But, as usual, Alicia was late. Luckily, Isolde was there to greet the board members as they came in. Nearly everyone in the room was much older than Isolde. But

they were gracious and seemed interested in Alicia's new pro-
tégé. They asked her questions about herself. She amped up her
professional biography somewhat, not of the things she'd done
here—they would surely know—but on the Austrian side. She
alluded to contacts in the European art world. This was the first
important meeting she'd been asked to attend and already it was
going so well. At one point, everyone in the room seemed to be
listening to her. Jokes were made about her youth and beauty. She
felt celebrated. But when Alicia arrived, Isolde could tell right away
that something was wrong. After the board meeting, Alicia asked
Isolde to come into her office and told her that she was letting her
go. Isolde was so shocked, she blurted out the first thing that came
into her mind.

"But you can't. You need me!"

"I'm sorry," Alicia said. "I think the chemistry's wrong."

"What chemistry? You haven't even given me a chance."

Now Alicia just looked at her, an unswerving gaze.

Isolde turned away and burst into tears.

She didn't even remember leaving Alicia's. Only later that night,
alone in her apartment, did it occur to her that she hadn't been paid
for the week she'd worked. Now that was really an injustice. She
had to be paid. She determined to show up the next day and insist
on getting the money that was her due.

The morning of the following day, Isolde rang Alicia's bell. The
maid answered over the intercom. There were several maids. This
one, Belén, seemed very young, just a girl, Isolde had thought, until
she'd learned one day that Belén had five children.

Ten minutes passed before Belén opened the front door of the building. But instead of letting Isolde come up as usual, she asked, clearly following orders, "How can I help you, Señora?"

"I've come for my salary," Isolde said.

Belén looked at her nervously. "Please wait," she said.

Isolde stepped inside to wait. It was humiliating, but she insisted on getting the money she deserved. There was not exactly a lobby, just a marble table with white-and-maroon swirls, a large mirror above it and a chair on either side. The chairs were purely decorative. They both faced out toward the door, not toward one another across the table. Clearly, no one was actually meant to sit here. All the furniture seemed to be sneering, whispering things like, You're not supposed to be here, You're not welcome, Anyone who enters will know you've been rejected.

A middle-aged man did enter, glancing at Isolde as he walked by. He turned back as he was nearing the elevators. "Can I help you?" he asked.

"No, no, thank you. I'm waiting for my friend."

After ten minutes, Belén reappeared. "Señora says she can't help you. Last week was a trial."

Isolde turned red. Here she was humiliated in front of the maid. "I won't leave unless I'm paid," she said.

"I'll be right back, Miss Isolde," Belén said.

Belén went back up and came down again. "You can come up and wait in the kitchen. Señora's in a meeting."

Isolde went upstairs. She sat with Belén in the kitchen. Belén was busily making empanadas. Alicia was obviously trying to humiliate her. Isolde felt many things, but overriding them all was the brute conviction, No matter what, I won't leave until I'm paid.

She waited twenty minutes, a half hour. She heard Alicia laughing in the other room, then, finally, someone leaving. Next Alicia took a call. After that, she rang the bell for Belén. Belén went to her. Another ten minutes passed. Belén returned to the kitchen and handed Isolde some bills. It was the weekly salary they had agreed upon. Isolde put the precious bills in her wallet.

"I'll go down with you," Belén said, as if afraid that Isolde would insist on seeing the Señora. Again, Isolde flushed red. She could find nothing to say. Belén of course knew everything, but what did she think? Her expression didn't betray a thing beyond nervousness. They went down in the elevator together. She must feel something, Isolde thought. She could imagine Belén telling the story to her friends, all of them putting their hands over their mouths, laughing. But she couldn't think about that. She'd got the money. It wasn't much, but she had to do what she could to make it last.

Alicia's building was walking distance from Isolde's house. At home, Claudia was making lunch. Isolde was glad to see her, to see someone. She was like this. When she felt badly, she wanted to be with people. She sat down at the table to wait until the lunch was ready.

"How's your father?" she asked Claudia.

"He's better," Claudia said. "He doesn't much like to take care of himself though. I said you have to stop drinking. He's drinking again. Poor guy. But what else is he going to do? His wife dead and children all gone."

She talked in her usual meandering way, her voice fading

in and out. This time Isolde didn't mind. But she couldn't help interrupting.

"You're married, right?"

"Yes. It's been two years."

"That's not so long."

"No."

"How old are you?" Isolde had imagined that, like Belén, all maids married young.

"Forty. When I was thirty-eight, I decided I wanted to have a baby. I had boyfriends, but boyfriends are no good. I needed to find a victim."

She had mumbled this last word. "A what?"

"A victim. I started looking around. Soon after that, I found him. He was the doorman in the building down the block. I started walking by there every day. I knew someone who knew him, another doorman, so I asked him to introduce us. From then on, whenever I walked by, we'd talk. One day, he asked me out."

Isolde laughed. "And he's your husband now?"

Claudia nodded, giggled.

"And is that okay?"

"He's a good husband. I knew he would be." She shrugged, went on working.

Isolde began eating her lunch. She felt suddenly uncomfortable in the presence of someone so sly whom she'd never imagined was sly at all.

There was a silence.

"The problem with you is that you trust too much," Claudia ventured.

Now Isolde really felt put out and she made it clear. "How do you know? Who do you know that I've ever trusted?"

Claudia shrugged, mumbled something.

Isolde went on eating. She felt furious on the one hand at Claudia's impudence, on the other, curious. What else did she know?

Claudia finished washing the dishes and started mopping the floor. Isolde eyed her.

"How did you know your husband was a victim?"

Claudia looked up. "You could see it in his face. Just look carefully. You can always tell."

Again Isolde bristled that Claudia would presume she needed this advice.

After lunch, Isolde went into the living room to do some calculations. She had to make her money last. How should she spend it? She counted the money she had along with the bills she'd just picked up. Her heart sank. Together it was so little.

Okay, calm down, she told herself. First things first. Beauty treatments were at the top of the list. The big art fair in Buenos Aires was opening that night. She had imagined going with Alicia. Now that wasn't possible, but she still had to go. She needed a wax and to do her nails. She stepped into the bathroom to review what she had, everything to do her nails, but she needed a new waxing kit.

She went down to the pharmacy on the corner. As she perused the aisles, hovering just below her—she tried not to lower her eyes—was a round dark pool of undulating water. She had been imagining that with this job her money woes were over. But how was she going to make money now? A thought occurred to her. She could even—she felt a sickening leap in her throat—get work in a beauty parlor, if all else failed. At least these were things she knew how to do. The undulating pool caught the light, widened. No, no, look away. She looked up, looked around. Was there no one? No one to help her, save her?

She returned to the apartment and went straight to work. Activity. Always the best thing in these moments. She had four things to do: her fingernails and toenails, the waxing of her legs and bikini line. Did she really need to wax her bikini line? Her legs, yes, of course. They would be bare. She was wearing the green-and-white-patterned skirt and the gold-and-silver sandals. Her feet were therefore crucial too. But was the bikini line necessary? Was someone really going to see her naked tonight? She sat back to think. What if she met one of those financial types who collected art? They had drinks and he wanted to take her home. She should say no, of course, hold on to her mystery. That's what the French girl would do. Maybe if Isolde simply didn't wax, that would force her to do what she knew she should do, not go home with anyone. But she couldn't trust herself. She knew what would end up happening. She would go home with the guy and, just to make it worse, would be all bristly. No, no matter what, she had to wax.

She tackled her toenails, removing the old polish, cutting back the cuticles. It was true. The activity did her good. She began to feel more hopeful. If she played it right, she might even find a new job tonight by schmoozing with the right people. She pictured herself entering the cocktail party—it was being held in La Rurale where, in the winter months, the big farm show was. The past year, in this very same space now filled with contemporary art, she'd walked through with Melody gazing at heifers, giant pigs. She pictured herself, smooth, seductive, exotic to her audience—she was aware of her charms. But everything had to look just right.

She stood up abruptly and looked in the mirror at her hair. Was it still okay? The roots were showing. They'd been showing slightly for a while, but now, in the warp of the mirror, they suddenly seemed to be showing much more. Or else her hair had had a growth spurt overnight. Her heart beat faster. She couldn't go to the party with her roots grown in like this. This was the moment she'd been dreading. If she couldn't color her hair anymore professionally, it was the beginning of the end. She'd determined to save all her money for this, even forgoing eating out. She was chubby anyway, she'd reasoned. But she'd also been counting on having a salary by now. She stopped what she was doing and went back to count her money. Doing her hair today would cost half of what she had. She could do it on a gamble, hoping to get a job tonight, but that was really crazy. She'd worked long enough in a bank to know.

The only other option was a home color treatment, but they made you look cheap, your hair all one color, uniformly. The way she had it done at the beauty parlor was strand by strand, highlights and lowlights. The result looked elegant. She examined her hair again. There was no question, it had to be done.

She went back down to the pharmacy. Standing outside it was a palo borracho tree covered with floppy pink blossoms. Since she'd been here earlier today, they'd started cutting it down. One man was up in the tree working with a chain saw, while the other directed from below. Already a number of branches, chopped up in large segments, were waiting on the sidewalk to be hauled away. Isolde entered the pharmacy, a condemned woman, she felt. She went to the aisle featuring hair products. She knew exactly where it was. The dyes were on the bottom. She had to squat down. Even the pictures on the outside of the boxes were horrible, the women's hair looked tinny. Was there really no other way? She thought again of selling off her jewelry.

But she'd already tried this. She'd taken her jewelry to several jewelry stores in her neighborhood, the idea being to sell a piece or two. But apart from one place on Quintana that bought a pair of earrings, no one else had been interested. She next tried the antiques shops in San Telmo. The prices they offered were ridiculous, of no use. So she'd kept her jewels and come back home. What was she anyway without her jewelry and clothes?

She brought the hair dye up to the counter, hoping to realize the transaction as quickly as possible, so as not to be seen by anyone she knew. Then she hurried home.

In the meantime, Claudia had gone out. Isolde was now alone. She closed herself in the bathroom and took out the dye. For a moment, despite herself, her interest was piqued, as with any beauty treatment. She had an interest in the mechanics of beauty, originating, no doubt, in her particular case, with her own beauty, but going beyond it. She read the instructions, looked up again at her hair. The next time she looked she'd be a crass, tinny blonde. From that point onward, she pictured her downward slide. She'd receive fewer and fewer invitations and finally only be invited to second-rung parties. More and more people, rather than turning to her as she entered a room, like flowers to the sunlight, as it seemed they sometimes did, would see her and turn the opposite way. Fewer men would want her on their arms. She pictured herself walking the streets, no one having offered her a ride and no longer having money for a taxi home. Then, again, what seemed to be the culminating shame, the job in the beauty parlor, kneeling down picking over someone's gnarly toes.

She shuddered. Surely it wouldn't come to that. She'd much rather slink home to her parents' house and wait it out there in her old bedroom. But an image crossed her mind of her crazy sister, doing just that. Then they'd really be a pair. Besides which, how could she ever afford the ticket home? Even that would be a problem. She'd have to work to buy a ticket so she could slink home.

Closed in the bathroom, the box of hair dye in her hand, she felt very afraid. In a moment, with a gesture, she would lose all her status. There was always the last option. Letting her hair grow out to its natural color. But that was impossible. The whole point was to be a blonde in this place. Everything depended on that. Again, like a torture, the image of herself working in a beauty parlor flashed into her head. She felt she couldn't breathe. She stepped out of the bathroom, put her hand to her chest, walked across the room. A set of French doors opened onto a balcony that looked down on the street below. Without willing it, another image entered Isolde's mind. She pictured throwing herself off that balcony, landing, dismembered, like the palo borracho branches, on the street below. She backed away from the French doors, gripping on to a chair.

At that moment, her cell phone rang. It rang once, twice, three times, unusual for her, since she usually answered right away. She stood reeling in the living room, holding on to the chair. Finally, she gathered herself enough to find her bag, tossed down earlier on the couch, reached inside and picked up her phone.

"Hello?" she said.

A man's voice answered. "Isolde, it's Enrique."

She scanned the men in her mind. Enrique? "Yes?" she said.

"I'm on the board of the Arts for Children committee. Do you remember, we exchanged a word the other day at the board meeting at Alicia's?"

She had a vague sense of who it might be, an older man with smooth white hair. He had asked her a few questions about her town in Austria. She had been vague, as she didn't like to reveal much about her past. But there had been a number of older men there. Maybe it was a different one.

"Hello, are you there?"

"Yes, yes," she said.

"Pardon me for calling your cell phone like this. It's the only number I was able to obtain for you. I'd be delighted if you'd accompany me to the art fair tonight."

She couldn't discern his motive. But she must do it, she told herself—pretending she was reluctant, though of course she wasn't—if it had anything to do with finding a job.

"Oh, well, yes, that would be fine."

"May I pick you up?"

She gave him her address, hung up. The apartment rippled before her eyes, as if consumed in haze, then righted itself.

Okay, good, she had an escort. Now what to do about her hair? She looked in the mirror again. She knew. She'd wear a headband, a wide black cloth one framing her face, covering the roots. It gave her an elegant, wealthy look. Yes, that was the answer, at least for now. She wouldn't dye her hair today.

twenty-three

I really needed a haircut and a wax. I also wanted to hear how Vera was doing. I got on that same bus I'd taken before, meandering through the city, a long woozy ride. We passed through the medical zone, an area full of hospitals and research centers. We passed the National Institute of Microbiology. Gabriel had told me about this place, a monumental building in the neoclassic style, designed by immigrant Italians. Inside were large quantities of snakes in crystal cages. They were brought in on the railroads—a big railroad station was nearby—so as to extract the venom needed to make vaccines. "Venom, like blood, can't be reproduced artificially," Gabriel said. He remembered vividly going there as a child. His friend's uncle, an employee, took the snakes out of the cages so they could touch them. "They were so cold," Gabriel said. In neighboring cages were the furry animals, rats and rabbits, reserved for the snakes' meals.

I got off the bus, pausing on the bridge as I walked over. It was near the end of the day. The light was hazy and warm and seemed to contain spores rising and falling. Or else it was pollution, I couldn't tell.

Vera was speaking in Belarusian to another woman when I arrived. I waved and sat down in the waiting area, flipping through the magazine *Gente* until Vera called me. She explained that the other woman was her friend and always did her waxing here.

"Her boyfriend's Muslim. He treats her really nice. She always takes all the hair off down there. She said that's what most Muslims do."

But Vera looked different. It was partly that she was tan.

"I called and you were at the beach," I said.

She was dressed up more than usual. She had earrings on. But it wasn't just that. She had a slightly harder look, maybe it was the eyeliner, black, right on the bottom rim of her eye. The jewelry also looked hard. She told me she had moved out. "A woman needs to be made to feel like a woman," she said. "I'm not talking about just having sex, but by the way he treats her. With my first husband, because of his illness, it became hard to have sex, but he still always made me feel like a woman."

By now, I had taken off my pants and was lying on the bed, which was covered with a sheet of paper. Vera was preparing the wax as she talked.

"How do you mean?"

"It could be anything. The touch of a hand as he was passing by." She was stirring the wax, thinking. "But maybe I idealize him." She swiped hot wax on my legs. "My daughter says I do. Something happened once. There was a hairdresser's on the ground floor of the apartment building where we lived. One time my husband told me he was going out to see a movie. This was strange. He never did this. But I was completely absorbed in the children, so I didn't care. Then a few weeks later my mother-in-law called me. We were good friends. She told me my husband was seeing a woman who worked at the hairdresser's. 'He's there now,' my mother-in-law said. 'Go find him.' I went. He was just leaving. But he lied and said that a woman there was the girlfriend of a friend of his. He'd had to give her a message. I believed him. But the next week I went to the hairdresser's myself to get a haircut. There was a pretty girl there working. I said, 'My mother-in-law says you're seeing my husband.' She pointed to the other girl beside her, who was ugly. "That's Tanya, not me.' I began talking to Tanya. She told me that my husband had lied to her, saying he was single. She had a lot of problems. She was single and had a daughter. They needed things. My husband had bought them for her. Then they'd gone out for coffee, started dating.

"After I was finished with my haircut, I invited her to come back to my house with me, so we'd both be there when Dima came home. Together, we packed up his things in a suitcase and waited there in the kitchen for him."

I laughed. "That's funny. Revenge."

"Of course." Vera looked at me quite seriously. "It's very important to take revenge. In the right way, of course. It doesn't mean you have to hurt anyone. But you act in a way that lets you keep your self-respect."

Yet another thing I'd never considered doing in my life, taking revenge.

"When Dima got home, we told him that his suitcase was all ready and he had to go. He went crazy. He lied about everything. Then Tanya left and he went after her. I found out later that he'd told her that he loved her, he wanted to be with her and didn't want to be with me. She said, 'No, forget it.' He came back and told me that he loved me and he didn't love her and all he wanted was to stay with me. The next day, I went to the hairdresser's again to talk to Tanya. She told me what he'd said, that he didn't want to be with me.

"That night, Dima came home. He said he wanted to do something very special, to have a special night together. He took me to the movies. Then he bathed me and made love to me, like never before, but I knew it was a lie. Later that night, when he was asleep, I went to the kitchen and took some pills, a lot of them. I didn't know how else to get out of the situation. He found me, passed out, and called an ambulance. I spent three days in the hospital, but they saved me. The doctor was furious, my daughter was still nursing. 'You were going to abandon your children for some man,' the doctor said. A psychiatrist came and told me to say I didn't want to kill myself, I just did it to scare my husband. Otherwise I would lose my job.

"That whole year, I was not myself. I didn't smile or laugh for a long time. My husband was really worried. He wouldn't even pass by the hairdresser's anymore. He'd take a bus on the other side of the building, wave as he was coming and going. I used to always be eating nuts. He would call me his squirrel. Now he would plead with me, saying, 'I want you to be like you were before, my little squirrel.' But I couldn't. To have been lied to like that was something I couldn't understand. Finally, I came out of it."

"You were able to forgive him?"

"I don't know if I forgave him. I just forgot. I became myself and we went on.

"A few years later, Tanya died. She'd had a kind of prostitute life. We wanted to adopt her baby. It was my idea. We tried, but it didn't work out. I don't know what happened to her."

Suddenly, she was laughing.

"Why are you laughing?"

"I'm just remembering, it was that year, the year that I started feeling better again, that the practice of blow jobs was imported to Belarus."

"What do you mean?"

"Yeah, no one did that. But then our friend Ludmila went to Poland with her husband, whose business had sent him there, and came back one day and told us about kissing everywhere on the body. None of us could believe it. I thought it was so disgusting that for months I couldn't eat off of Ludmila's plates. Just the thought of her eating off those same plates made me sick. Then little by little, we all started trying it."

twenty-four

The botanist wrote me. He was even more excited. The latest news was that they were launching a massive counterattack on the *Iris pseudacorus* invasion, a measure known as biological control.

In a biological control scenario, natural enemies such as insects, fish and pathogens are purposefully introduced by scientists to weaken and suppress invading plants. In order to find the right biological control agent, scientists travel the world in search of the target plant's natural enemies. Once found, the weakening agent is imported to the host country and placed in a quarantine laboratory. There, meticulous experiments are carried out to ensure that the organism will affect only the invading species and will not impact native or crop species.

Next the enemy agent is released into its new habitat to prey upon the invader. Classical biological control relies on numerous generations of the enemy agent to suppress the invading species over a long period of time. Another method, inundative biological control, functions through vigorous and swift counterattack, with enemy agents released en masse.

In this case, inundative measures were being taken. Vast quantities of mottled weevils had been released in the wetlands. Simultaneous intergenerational damage was hoped for with the adults feeding on the leaves, where they would produce characteristic feeding scars, and the larvae tunneling in the petioles and crown of the plant. While the plants would not be wiped out immediately, their vigor would be considerably compromised, with the youthful irises suffering particularly.

I called Leonarda. "Whatever happened with that dinner with the Beast?"

"Really? You want to do it?"

"Why not? I'm hungry."

"Okay, great."

I knew it would be something absurdly laborious, baby ducks steeped in wine for several days prior, then cooked low for twelve hours. Whatever. The perfect aperitif, wine, digestif. I relished all this preoccupation.

We settled on that coming Thursday at 9:00 P.M. I snuck into the back garden a bit before that, positioning myself against the wall by the kitchen window, pressed into the jasmine.

Inside, there was an immense amount of fastidious bustling. Leonarda was wearing green corduroys with a short skirt on top. She disappeared for a little while and came back transformed, the skirt alone, little heels, a blouse with a ruffle.

I knelt there, breathing in the jasmine. At 9:30, she called me. I was holding my vibrating phone in my hand.

"Hiiiiiiiii. We're waiting for you."

At 10:00, she said, "Where the hell is she?" She was angry and flounced petulantly around the house.

"Let's start anyway," Miguel said from the stove.

"I don't want to start," Leonarda said.

He had already poured them aperitifs.

He turned back to the stove. He was stirring. "Well, the risotto can't wait. It'll be ruined."

Suddenly, he looked agitated. He started moving his feet up and down, as if the floor were too hot.

She glanced over with a look of scorn. "What's wrong with you?"

He pulled the pan off the fire. He was quivering, seemingly in a state of uncontrollable fury. This, at least, was amusing. She laughed. She went over to look in the pan.

"It's already ruined," he said. The tendons on his neck and fore-arms were standing out.

She dipped her finger in, tasted, wrinkled her nose in an awful way.

He threw his hands up violently in the air, turned and left the room.

She called me again. The phone vibrated outside, stirring the jasmine, right at my wrist. It was 10:30.

She walked into the living room where he was wobbling on the couch, smoking his pipe, visibly strung out.

"This is weird. I think something's up. I'm going to her house." She had put short boots on instead of her heels.

She left.

A moment after the door closed, he got up. He went into the kitchen and threw the risotto out. He took the ducks out of the oven, poured himself some wine and ate some snails. Then he put a

DVD into his computer and sat down at his desk to watch it. Leonarda had told me that he liked to watch American TV series, like *Sex and the City*. He gradually relaxed. Every now and then he laughed.

I closed my eyes and rested the back of my head against the wall.

After a little while, Leonarda returned. Now she was the one in a state. "What the fuck? She's not there. I went inside and everything."

"You went in?"

"Yeah, I have the key."

He set about warming up the meal. "Let's eat," he said.

She flung herself down at the table.

"Have some wine," he said.

She didn't touch her wine. I was enjoying this. She hardly touched her food, pulled the snails out of their shells curiously, as if it were an experiment, and left them lying there on her plate.

"I'm not hungry," she said after a while. She got up and left the table.

He didn't say anything, though his silence seemed to require considerable control, poured himself some more wine, finished his meal.

My mouth was watering as I watched. Finally, he got up and walked down the hall toward the bathroom. She was nowhere in sight, must have retreated to the kid's room.

The window by the table was open onto the garden. She had hardly touched her baby duck. Dare I? I leaned in and plucked the bird off her plate. I carried it across the grass to the little bench in the far corner of the garden, where I sat down and ate it swiftly with my hands.

twenty-five

At first, she felt queasy. She was holding her breath, trying not to smell things. She had sought out a place as far away as possible from her usual stomping ground, so she wouldn't have to run into anyone she knew. This neighborhood was literally outside the city. She'd also taken the extra precaution of wearing a wig, sleek, black, shoulder-length, with bangs.

At first, she kept her distance from the other women there. But she couldn't help overhearing their conversations, and then following them from day to day. One woman in particular narrated things very well.

The day she'd hired her, the owner, Juana, had asked, "What do you do?"

"Makeup and hands," she'd said.

There wasn't much makeup work, so she began with hands. She did her first few pairs with repugnance, holding her breath. Then one day she worked a miracle on a pair of fingernails, making these ugly things—they'd been a particularly ugly pair, long, dirty, cracked—beautiful. Okay, she thought, think of it that way. The work required confronting ugliness, making it beautiful. This was something she could understand.

Another day a woman came in with her daughter. It was the

daughter's fifteenth birthday. They both needed makeup. Juana called her over.

She was nervous, but everything she put on the girl made her look so pretty that she gained confidence. Next she did the mother. Everyone in the beauty parlor exclaimed at her skill. "Now we don't even know who's the mother and who's the daughter," they said. One of the girls working there was going out on an important date that night. "Hey, can you make me up?" she asked.

Going home on the bus that night, Isolde felt so happy she wanted to shout. Then she caught herself and felt strange, as if she must be living in a warped world. Could that really make her so happy, to put makeup on a working girl in a remote, shitty corner of a Third World city? She shrugged. Well, it had. The feeling was there, solid, in her stomach.

It is said that monkeys are drawn instinctively to hair. The pleasure that the touch of hair affords them is such that they seek it from any source, the dead as well as the living, strangers as well as their own kind. Any hairy object, animate or inanimate, may form the subject of their investigations. The pleasure is the pleasure of the fingers. The specific life of the hand begins with grooming.

Her entire life Isolde had had a horror of hair. Everyone in her family knew this. A hair on the sink, on the table, not to mention on the food. When she had been little and came across a hair in an unexpected place, she would start to cry. Sometimes she would even cry for a long time. To avoid these scenarios, her family would whisk any loose hairs away as soon as they appeared.

One day, Juana came over as Isolde was working on someone's

feet. "We're going to have to teach you to wax," she said. Isolde's face must have betrayed something. "The way we work here is that we all know how to do everything," Juana said. But still she didn't press Isolde right away.

The next few nights, lying in bed, Isolde thought about hairs, meshes of them, creeping, crawling over everything. Dark or pale, white blond against pink skin or reddening at the roots. Hairs that had been dyed and were growing out white. Patches of flesh overgrown with hairs. She felt suffocated, pictured hair growing inside her throat, like a thicket, prickly, blocking the whole passage, encroaching on her tongue.

While before she'd avoided even looking at the activities in the beauty parlor that had to do with hair, now she began to pay quiet attention. She knew she had to conquer this fear of hair. She began sweeping up the hair left on the floor after a cut. She'd been amazed that the other women could eat their lunches in this place so full of hair. She'd always step outside to eat herself, sitting on the bench right by the front door. One day, she made herself eat inside with them. She had to learn to be around hair.

That same afternoon, Juana asked her to wash a woman's hair before a cut. It gave Isolde goose bumps, but she managed it. Soon afterward, Vera said one morning when Isolde arrived, "Today I'm going to teach you how to wax." A few hours later, a young woman came in. She had tawny skin and hair almost the same color. "Come on," Vera said, waving her hand at Isolde with an impish smile. Isolde went into the little back room with Vera and the woman. Vera explained how to heat and stir the wax. She let Isolde stir, waiting for the moment when the wax was liquified but not transparent. Vera spread wax on the woman's leg and then tapped it with a wooden spatula. Once it was hard, but not too dry, she tore it off. The woman cried out. Her skin was left rosy and uncannily smooth.

The mechanics of waxing were not foreign to Isolde. She did know, after all, how to wax herself. But she still wasn't prepared for the first client she had, a dark-haired woman with lots of hair, not only on her legs and in her armpits, but everywhere, even on the fleshy curves of her butt. She had never seen so much hair on a woman in her life.

Isolde plunged in. Unlike the first woman, who had cried out, this woman was used to the treatment. She made little grunts, nothing more, as the hair was ripped out. Isolde was sweating, she kept working. Whichever way the woman turned, there seemed to be more hair. Vera checked in on her every ten minutes.

Finally, once it was over and the woman had left, Isolde sat down, flushed and exhausted. Juana brought out a bottle of champagne. "To celebrate your first waxing," she said.

Over time, Isolde actually began to find the waxing satisfying. It even felt like a way for her to actively engage her lifelong horror of hair. Through actions of her own, she could confront and conquer it. She delighted in the smooth, clean surface of the skin afterward. The wonder of the wax, the hairs suddenly all gone.

It was also strangely satisfying to get up every day and have something particular to do, somewhere to go, rather than have the whole day there, shapeless, looming before her. She was less lonely. She was in the company of people all day, listening to chatter, hearing stories. It helped that her clientele weren't the kind of people she knew. They were from the province of Buenos Aires, Avellaneda.

She still went to cocktail parties in the evenings. Of course, she could get any kind of beauty treatment done now for free. If anything, her look was now even sleeker, with the constant touch-ups. She received offers for dates, went on dates. She still handed out her card at cocktail parties, though less frequently.

A t first, I only knew that Isolde called me less. I called her myself, to find out if everything was all right. When I did see her, she seemed different. I wasn't sure if this was good or bad, but I did notice that I felt more relaxed around her. She was less bubbly. You didn't feel you had to muster the same energy.

Then it happened. One day at the beauty parlor, I noticed a new woman working. I saw the back of her head, shiny black shoulder-length hair. She turned. I saw only a sliver of her face, but I recognized her movement. Then she stood up and walked away. The walk. It was dizzying—it could only be Isolde.

But I held back my impulse to call out her name. Something was obviously going on. She was here in disguise, didn't want to be discovered. I followed Vera into the little back room.

"There's a new girl?" I asked.

"Yeah, an Austrian," Vera said. "At first, she didn't speak at all. She was very cold. But she learned quickly. She has a certain touch, and a stylish look, which Juana likes." Vera smiled. "Now she's changing, loosening up a little bit."

The black hair actually looked great on Isolde, giving her a different air of sophistication.

When I came out of the waxing room, black-haired Isolde was coming right toward me, leading a woman to the pedicure area. We made eye contact. There was no way to avoid it. She started.

"Hey," I said, softly.

She put her finger to her lips. I nodded. I was getting a pedicure with Vera. It was near the end of the day. When I finished and stood up to pay, Isolde walked by me again. "Wait for me in the café at the end of the block," she whispered.

I did as she'd said. About twenty minutes later, she came in. This had been her nightmare, being discovered. But now that it had happened, she was matter-of-fact. She sat down and took her wig off. Her blond hair was pulled back tight in a ponytail, then looped up at the base of her neck. She pulled off the ponytail holder and shook it out. Watching her, I admired her practicality.

"So," she said, "what are you doing all the way out here?"

I told her about the first day I'd come to look at the Riachuelo and how I'd met Vera.

"Now I come back to see her," I said.

"Yeah, she's nice," Isolde answered. "She tells good stories."

She seemed a bit tired. Her nails were freshly done. She looked up at me and smiled. Suddenly, the voice was back, melodious, the accent. "There's an opening at Benzacar tonight, a new artist, should be interesting. Would you like to join me?"

"Sure, why not?" I said, both impressed and thrown, not least by the trace of irony in her eyes.

She glanced at what I was wearing. "If you come home with me now, you can borrow some clothes."

I looked down at what I was wearing, an outfit that up to then had seemed perfectly fine to me. "Okay," I agreed.

twenty-six

Night fell rapidly. Leonarda and I were prowling around. I flashed my teeth at her in the dark.

"I think it's time to tell you," I said.

"Tell me what?"

"What I'm doing here."

"What do you mean, what you're doing here?"

"Well, I actually work in intelligence," I said.

"Ha-ha. That's the stupidest thing I've ever heard. And that's coming from someone stupid."

"Think about it. Why else would I be here?" I countered.

This seemed to hit home. Her weak spot, the national inferiority complex. Why would anyone come to Argentina?

Cars were whizzing by us, shaking up the flowering trees. Just then my cell phone beeped, indicating it was low on battery.

"What's that?" She glanced around quickly. Miss Techie to boot. It was almost like a caricature. That's right, of course, I thought, she's pathologically paranoid.

"No, nothing," I said.

I laughed. In that moment, I remembered something else that Canetti says, this time about laughter. "A human being who falls down reminds us of an animal we might have hunted and brought down ourselves. Every sudden fall that arouses laughter does so because it suggests helplessness and reminds us that the fallen can, if we want, be treated as prey. We laugh instead of eating it."

I was working to destabilize her in one way or another.

She hadn't lasted long living at the guy's place, which wasn't to say that she was through with him. She'd found lodging in a house with several other young women. "Come visit me," she said. "I have the cutest little room."

I timed it so that I was on my way out for the evening. I was meeting up with Pablo, the guy I'd met that night in the bar with Gabriel.

"Can I take a shower?" I asked. I took a shower in the little bathroom off her room. I came back out. "Do you have anything lacy?"

"Why?"

I shrugged. "Just to look nice. I have a meeting."

She stood, opened a drawer, looked through her clothes. She was clearly unhappy and not adept at hiding it.

I tried on one negligee after another and finally decided on a purple one.

"You like that one?" she said. "Good. Let's go."

"What do you mean?" I laughed.

"Let's go, I'm going with you." She gripped the back of my neck with her hand.

I shrugged her off, laughing, started putting eyeliner on in the mirror. "I wish I could bring you," I said. "But I can't."

That encounter gave me an idea. Her place was centrally located. At every possible opportunity, whether she was there or not, I would stop by on my way out for the evening. I would use her bathroom. I would pee or take a shower, drying off with her towel. My excuse was always that the water wasn't working at my place. I would use her deodorant, her perfume. Or if I had perfume with me, I would spray it around. Once I even touched myself and left a snail trail on her washcloth.

Silly as they might sound, these gestures were satisfying me. With each one, I wriggled freer from the trap.

Her bras didn't fit me, but once I borrowed some underwear, leaving a pair of mine in her dirty-clothes basket. I left a trace of lipstick on the sheet. A few blond hairs in her hairbrush, contrasting markedly with her dark ones. I shaved my armpits with her razor.

The idea was to scatter pheromones around. I kept a litany in my head of the substances containing pheromones: snail trail, spit, snot, perfume, sweat, pee.

If she was there, I would lie back on the bed, stretch my arms out, baring my armpits.

"This guy I'm meeting tonight is a writer, quite good, I think. At least, he has original ideas."

Sometimes I would actually be meeting someone—I had picked up the habit of going to that bar and occasionally going home with someone. At other times, as in this case, it was a lie.

"What do you know about original ideas?" she snapped.

What mattered was that I had captured her attention in a

new way. Her energy, usually so diversified, was caught and she with it, here in this little cage of a room. The key, of course, was that I had somewhere to go. I had no delusions, the whole situation was predicated on that. If I was fleeing, she had no need to.

"Oops, it's late," I said, sitting up.

twenty-seven

One day, as she was coming home from the beauty parlor, Isolde's downstairs neighbor, a man in his forties, asked. "Would you like to come in for a cup of tea?"

Isolde was taken aback, which made her answer somewhat brusquely. "Oh, no, no, I can't. Thank you." She couldn't imagine any interest in having tea with this man. In fact, a moment later as she was opening her apartment door, she had a hard time even recollecting his face. Was he that nondescript or simply off her radar?

The guy didn't mention it until a month had passed, when he asked again, "Would you accept my tea today?"

His timing was propitious. Isolde had had a hard day. She was tired. Her hands were tired. She'd been working with them all day. Her legs were tired. She was someone who liked company. She went in and sat with him. In a moment, she would continue on up to her apartment, get dressed for the cocktail party she meant to go to, but for now she would rest.

The guy, Hernán, had untidy brown hair that fell into his eyes. He put music on. He was cooking. He seemed to feel that was enough, to be in each other's presence, cooking with the music on. Usually, Isolde would have felt uncomfortable with such a lack of chatter but, after the daylong chatter at the beauty parlor, silence was a relief. And the smell and sound of food cooking. He had a comfortable chair with cushions. She let herself sink into it.

After that, from time to time, she'd stop in and have tea with him at the end of her day. Once tea led to dinner. He was actually a good cook, surprising in an Argentine man. Except for the barbecue, which was a field of macho competition, very few Argentine men she'd met could cook.

Now and then he mentioned a friend, but it seemed that, on the whole, he lived in his own world. He didn't seem to expect her to invite him to her place or to do anything really. He didn't ask her any troubling questions about her life. He was not much of a talker in general. But she could feel how content he was with her presence. One day it occurred to her to wonder what he liked about her. Certainly not the things she would imagine a person would like about her. She never acted like her glamorous self in front of him. She was often tired, never dressed up, hardly bothered to charm. And she certainly wasn't supplying sexual favors. They hadn't so much as brushed hands in passing.

She didn't mind his seeing her going out to a party dressed to the nines, as he sometimes did, but she was embarrassed that he would know what kind of work she did. She didn't tell him. He didn't ask. Then one day she found herself simply talking about something that had happened in the beauty parlor, something funny, it came tumbling out. It must have been that she was feeling so comfortable. In any case, it didn't seem to matter. He enjoyed her story, listened and laughed, and didn't seem in the least surprised about where she worked. Had he known it all along? She didn't ask, simply left it at that.

One day, playing, she showed up in her black wig. "That looks nice on you," he said.

"Do you prefer dark-haired women or blondes?"

He shrugged. "Either way. I like both."

"Oh, come on, that's impossible. You must have a type."

He shrugged. "Not really. Take you. You look great both ways."

Another day, she inadvertently discovered that his mother was institutionalized. In and out of depression for most of her life, she had tried to kill herself the year Hernán had turned thirty. She hadn't succeeded, only enough to turn herself into a vegetable. "Probably better that way, poor thing," he said. "She seems to suffer less." He had grown up with her, his father gone, though it was from his father's side that he'd come into the rental properties, a few apartments, some Chinese grocery stores. One of them was this apartment where he lived now. The others generated enough for him to live off the rents.

Once after a particularly harrowing day—she'd had a prostitute client who'd kept falling asleep as Isolde was doing her nails, then waking and saying that she didn't like the color, so that Isolde had had to start all over again—Isolde stayed on later than usual at Hernán's.

"Here," he said, seeing how tired she was, "why don't you lie down?" She let him put her in his bed, take off her shoes. She turned away and collapsed, her blond hair on the pillow. Hernán sat across the room in an armchair, watching her for a while.

Isolde woke, surprised, looked over, alarmed. But she was still in her clothes, while he, also fully clothed, slept soundly in the armchair. She felt a first flush of feeling for him in that moment. It frightened her. It seemed so enigmatic and not at all attached to any of the reasons she'd imagined a person would love another, that she crept out without waking him as quickly as she could.

After that experience, she stayed away for a week or more. He didn't press her. When she finally came down again to visit him, she had a different awareness. Maybe it was this she'd been afraid of, that had been keeping her at bay. She watched him cook. She noticed everything, the way his hair dipped to one side at the back of his neck, his smell. As she watched, she wondered, does he have girls? Then she remembered. She'd seen him often with a girl in the early days, small, cute, dark-haired. What had happened with her?

"What happened to that girl you were always with?" she asked.

He looked over his shoulder. "Sofia? We didn't fit together," he said. "I was trying to force it, but we didn't fit."

That night, Isolde went back upstairs, but as she lay in bed, her mind on Hernán, she began to feel impatient. She got up and went back downstairs in her nightgown. He'd been sleeping but, seeing her at the door, he took her hand quite simply and led her inside. For some reason, she'd imagined that he wouldn't know what to do with a woman but, to her surprise, he actually seemed quite knowledgeable on the subject.

twenty-eight

The grant people wrote again. My time was almost up. They were expecting my final report, at which point I'd receive the last installment of money. I printed out my half-term report, gathered the rest of my notes and lay them out all around me on the floor. I wasn't at all sure that I'd collected the kind of information they wanted. Nor was I sure how to present it.

I wrote an e-mail to my friend Brian to get some pointers about presentation and in the meantime settled down to work.

Gabriel rang the bell as I was dozing on the floor in my sea of notes.

"Oh, boy," he said, seeing papers all over the floor, "what're you up to?"

"Writing my water report," I said. "What about you?"

"A funny thing just happened. A guy just wanted to watch me typing naked. Yeah, I swear. He brought his computer with him. For one hour and he gave me a hundred pesos."

"Sounds great," I said. "Do you think that could work for me? I could type up my report and make some money in the process."

"Of course," he said. "You just have to find the right person." He sat down in his favorite spot on the chaise lounge. "How's everything else going?" he asked.

"Good." I smiled.

"Wait, you're up to something."

"Yeah," I said, sitting down across from him. "I figured out a way to get my revenge. I'm attacking Leonarda, without her knowing it. It's cool, I swear, I sort of have her in my power."

"You're kidding."

"No, really, I can't believe it. It's like she's my little prey now. I came to the conclusion that it's the only way to deal with her, the only thing she'll respond to. She's gripped, she's totally gripped."

"What's the secret?"

"Simple, really. I realized I just need to have a second life besides her, somewhere else to go. Sometimes I really do have somewhere to go. I go to that bar we went to."

"No kidding."

"Yeah, I've been taking your advice about getting more sex in my life."

"You pick up people?"

"Sometimes. But often I don't. I just go home. Still I pretend to her that I have a date. It's the need to leave. If you're always fleeing, she doesn't have to."

He paused for a moment.

"It sounds like you're enjoying this."

"I am. But mainly I feel like I've broken free. I'm not in her power anymore."

There was a flicker in Gabriel's eye. Was it doubt? I registered it, but only took the time to think about it much later on.

"And what about Miguel?" he asked.

"Out of the picture. As far as I know. But now I don't even care."

"I can see that, comparatively speaking, your water report might be less than compelling."

"Yeah, well." I looked down at the sea of papers again.

Outside, dusk was falling. Silky darkness creeping in. Soon I would be on my way.

I slithered through the night, reptile-like, gleaming. A crocodile in the waterways of the city, traveling along the underground streams, surfacing when I reached my destination, crawling up, scales shining.

She would wait. She had indeed a furry-animal look. She'd be wearing a T-shirt and corduroys, eyes wary and eager at the same time.

"Hi."

"Hi."

She was sitting on her bed. There was nothing else in her room but the little bed. I couldn't believe it. She, so fleeting and squeamish before, was now here waiting, a furry prey under my dominion, finally, after all that, in my grasp.

I shook myself, the water dripping off my scales.

"I brought you something," I said. I gave her a little pink-ribboned bag. In it was one of those mini chocolate cakes she loved.

"Oh!" She was happy.

She looked at me as she bit into the cake. This too was new. She, queen of action, was now watching, waiting to see what I would do.

I sat down. Very delicately, I pulled her dark hair aside and bit the back of her neck. First the sound she made, strangled, surprised, seemed genuine, then, as I moved my mouth farther down, biting along the tender muscles, she began to groan. It sounded like the groan she thought she was supposed to make, that she'd learned in the movies.

"Shh," I said.

She shut up, surprised.

There was a moment of awkwardness. In an attempt to combat it, she turned and pulled her shirt up, offering her breasts to me. Her breasts, weighty, womanly, with their submerged blue veins, belying the girlishness of the rest of her form. In another moment, I would have eaten them hungrily, but that was not the plan. I stood up and smiled.

"I only have a moment today," I said.

"Wait!" Breasts bobbing.

I waved and turned away. Tempt and torture, that was my idea.

The next time I came by, she was wearing a robe. She had put on false eyelashes. The pair on the left side now hung by a thread.

She was quiet, waiting, breathing. Her shallow breath was raucous. I had her lie down and moved my hands over her back. Her body, I could feel it, was very tense. This was difficult for her, I knew, to lie there and let herself be touched. But, while on other occasions she'd squirmed away, now she let me. I brushed the hair back from her forehead, caressed her sleek, shining seal head, the same caress over and over again. Very, very gradually, I felt her relax.

Then I lay down with her on the bed and held her until I had to go again.

The next time, I decided to try something else. I gripped her wrists behind her and turned her over. She was wearing violet underwear and I pulled them down. Her nimble little butt shone. I spanked her. She cried out in surprise, squirmed. The rosiness spread. She grew still again, waiting for more.

Each time beforehand, I imagined in my mind's eye what I would do. Once I found a notebook. She too was keeping a record, writing down, each time, what we had done.

Sometimes the street outside her little room was silent, sometimes it was filled with a throng. I pictured a thronging mass on the cobblestones.

She had decorated the room, put a colored scarf over the light. She must have been touching herself before I arrived. Her pussy glistened in the colored light. It looked swollen, pinkish, reminding me of a mouth smudged with lipstick after it's been kissed. All over Buenos Aires you see that, in the plazas, on the streets, the smudged mouths of women and teenage girls. I remember especially the jeering, smudged mouth of a girl who rushed past me out of a plaza, hands high in the air. She seemed to have achieved some victory by being kissed, was advertising it to the world.

A fragile shower of pollen was settling over the streets when I stepped out, like the fine gold dust on the inner edge of her ear, which I had rubbed off with a finger.

"Are they dirty?"

"You should clean them."

She started to get up. I pressed her back down. "Not now."

We were lying there quietly. Finally, after all this time together, we could be quiet. I had a longing to stay, but I knew I couldn't.

Outside on the streets everything trembled, the flowering trees shook. I walked calmly through the city, though the noise of the buses was jarring and the fetid smell in some spots nearly overwhelming. People brushed against me, jostled me, seemingly trying to exasperate me, but it didn't work.

I chose my path, at the opportune moment slunk underground, glided along the waterways. I would have preferred not to leave, to stay the night with her, but I knew it was impossible. My staying would have destroyed everything, shattered the cage, she would have been gone in a flash. I had been ingenious enough to find a way to trap her, of this I was proud. I had a certain power over her now, which was not entirely satisfying, but it was satisfying enough. Much better than not seeing her at all, which I couldn't have borne.

twenty-nine

Early on in *Madame Bovary*, there's a passage devoted to Charles and Emma's love in the early months of their marriage. Here we have a vision of how the story could have ended, this young love deepening, if Emma had been able to continue to love Charles, instead of growing bored, yearning for something else.

From a double, Isolde soon found that she had a triple life. She wouldn't think of asking Hernán to her cocktail parties, couldn't imagine him fitting into that world. When she was thinking in this vein, she felt repugnance. He wasn't good enough for her. He wasn't sophisticated. Sometimes even the smell of him bothered her.

On the other hand, she began to feel a sweetness to her days, a slight ripple of happiness at the thought of coming home from the beauty parlor, knowing she could knock on his door and find him there. She felt comforted knowing that she could call him, at any moment in the course of her day, and he would always pick up the phone. Sometimes she'd call just for that reason, checking to see if he was still there. He seemed to understand that that was why she'd called and it didn't bother him. No matter what she did, he seemed touched and amused by her.

The sweetness of repetition—she'd call as she was leaving the beauty parlor to let him know when she'd be home. He'd have something nice waiting for her, a snack or a cocktail. She'd tell him about her day. If she was in a talkative mood, she could go into as much detail as she wanted, and Isolde could go into exhaustive detail, or, if she didn't feel like talking, she simply wouldn't. The music would be on.

She had never been near someone, not really. It was completely strange to her. She marveled at how he so simply included her. The loneliness that she had become familiar with—it had been perhaps the one constant in her life—was gone. The longing that went hand in hand with the loneliness was also gone. She felt that although she had been surrounded by people—she had always, somewhat frantically, been surrounded by people—she had been alone her whole life until now.

One day, he showed her one of his other rental properties, a larger place. "Too good for me," Hernán said. "I'd never live here on my own." She looked around. It wasn't stunning, but it was nice enough. "But the two of us could live here," he said. "You wouldn't have to work." For a moment, her repulsion rose up again. Move in with him? What was he thinking? But in the weeks that followed, she found herself decorating the new place in her mind.

thirty

I have to finish this up. I need you to come," Leonarda said.

"Sure, why not?" I answered.

"Just one last time. Then we'll be done with him."

Dinner with the Beast, take two. Otherwise known as the final act of the Master Plan. He had cooked us an elaborate meal. I watched the flashing of the forks and knives. The living creature is always soft and vulnerable somewhere. I looked at his bald head, her short neck. Someone here will be prey. Where were we each the most fleshy? I turned and eyed her quickly, in case she was up to something. But she wasn't paying attention. Her nose was crinkled up.

I noticed it too, a smell, almost like meat rotting in the early stages, beginning to turn. It was faint. I didn't say anything. But then Leonarda got up and said, "I think there's something bad in your fridge."

She went to the refrigerator and started looking over things.

"Hey, stop that, eat your meal," he said.

She was bent over, her butt in the air. "Yes, Daddy," she said. She turned and looked over her shoulder—"We decided we're both calling you 'Daddy' today"—and went on looking, lifting up one thing after another and smelling it. She found something and held it out. It looked like a bag of greens, Italian parsley.

"How can parsley smell so bad?" she said. Although it did look sort of liquified. "There must be something else." She began poking around some more.

"Okay, okay, enough," he said. He took the parsley bag from her hand, put it in the trash, took the trash bag out of the can and placed it outside the door. "Now can we eat?"

"I'd be delighted to," she said.

There was tension between them, but it was of a different kind than before. It seemed her fascination with him, or with her fantasy of him, the big game she'd been after, had waned. In its stead was something else, a sort of charged repugnance. He had been her prey. Her interest had been in the pursuit, in tracking and seizing her quarry. Now that she had succeeded, she didn't seem to have much interest in eating him. But it was not only that. There was also disappointment. He had surrendered too fully. She had told me on the way there that in their last encounter he had gotten down on his knees, begged her to marry him. Could it be true? He said she was a coward, she was denying something big if she refused him. She would regret it to the end. Again, the island came up, the island he would buy for her in Tigre.

He cared so much that she liked his food. But she wasn't eating. I felt for him, a pang. There was nothing worse she could do to him than not finish his food.

She pushed her plate back. "This was so fun before. Now it's ruined."

"Why ruined?" he asked, in his radio announcer voice. He seemed to be attempting to make it emanate off the walls. But nothing worked anymore. He had to be great to warrant her humiliating him. His greatness alone, imagined or real, made it satisfying. When she didn't answer, he chewed on his lip, rabbit-like, yet another specimen of small game, the streets outside full of such rabbit-like game, chewing on pale grasses. It was this that made her furious, that he was like the rest.

"Stop doing that!" He stopped, which seemed to irritate her even more. She stood up. "I'm going."

"Wait." We both said it, he and I in tandem.

"I wanted to open a bottle of wine, a very special bottle," he said.

"Oh, you with the wine," she said, rolling her eyes. But it was clear that this had had an effect.

"A Saint Emilion from '76. It was written up recently."

"In your wine magazine?" she asked with condescension. There was a wine magazine that he sometimes wrote for. He had managed to make her curious, but she still pretended to be bored, in a juvenile, boyish way. "Okay, I'll have a sip before I go."

He took tiptoe ballerina steps to the kitchen, as if any brusque move might make her leave.

I knew that, as always, the best thing was to distract her. I picked up one of his pipes from the windowsill. I lit it, puffed. She laughed.

He reappeared, wine bottle in hand. "Come this way," he said, wisely changing the setting.

We migrated to the living room. He had opened the wine, was letting it breathe. I kept the pipe in my hand. It was evident, from her demeanor, that the tide had changed. Always, when she perked up, she was like a child. It was so easy to make her happy. He and I caught each other's eye—here she was, happy again.

The night went on. The guards crossed the garden. We sipped the wine. She disappeared for a moment, then came out eating a slender bit of ham, pink and delicate, carved from the spit. She put her head back and let it drop into her mouth. He was watching her mutely. The ridiculous, hilarious thought occurred to me, he wants to be eaten like that ham.

Suddenly, she was excited. "I had an image, I had an image," she said to him. "I came over, I was spying on you from the garden. You were here, right here, down on your hands and knees with another guy, biting each other's necks like dogs."

Eyes on her, he slowly got down on his hands and knees. Her nostrils flared, watching. There was a sense that he was obliging her, like a father does a child. Is he a little jaded? He's too old for this. Or is that precisely the point? He's sensing this will be his last round of fun.

She stepped nearer, was standing over him. The surge of power, she the survivor standing over her victim, this at least still captivated her.

"Okay," she said, "now we're going to tie you up."

He started to stand, but she pressed him down with her foot.

"Get some rope," she said to me. "Hey, Daddy, where's the rope?"

I found some rope, under the sink. He let himself be tied. I had worked on boats for a summer, so knew how to tie a knot. I did it well, his hands behind his back, his knees and ankles together.

He was down on his knees tied up before her. "At least let me suck you," he said in that marvelous voice.

I didn't think she was going to do it, but she slowly undid her pants, lowered her purple flowered underwear.

We left him tied up there. I didn't care at the time. I felt nauseous, like I'd had an overdose of something. On the street, Leonarda and I parted somewhat brusquely. The truth was I wanted to get away from her. I was thinking how lovely it would be to meet up with some nice girl or boy and go out for an ice cream or dance a slow dance in my kitchen.

But a few days later, I started to wonder about Miguel, tied up there. Another day passed. I checked the Internet to see how long you could survive without water. I knew how good those knots were.

On the evening of the fourth day, I decided to go over to his house, just to reassure myself. I took a taxi. Dusk was falling. We passed a police car on the way. Suddenly, I had an image of his building surrounded by police cars.

But when I got there, there were no police cars. The building was quiet. I went in, nodding to the doorman as I passed. It was the chubby one with bristly hair, he knew me. I rang Miguel's bell and waited. No answer, no sound. I rang again. Nothing.

Instead of leaving the premises, I slipped through the door at the far end of the lobby into the night garden. There was the smell of the jasmine, woozily strong. But then another smell too, putrid. I crept nearer to his windows. They were dark and closed. But the smell was stronger here. We had chased down the prey, caught and tied him up, and then allowed him to rot. The prey? What was I thinking, using this language? He was a man, with whom I had talked, shared meals. He'd actually been quite kind to me.

It was all coming back. The way Leonarda had turned out the lights before leaving. Also the gag at the last minute. She had handed me her scarf and told me to gag him. Thinking now, it seemed like madness.

I had been keeping a journal about our adventures from the beginning. I had written about our hunting games. And about my jealousy. Suddenly it occurred to me—they would find my journal and use it as evidence. Leonarda had also been writing things down. I could never decipher what they said because of her crabbed writing, but surely they were even more incriminating.

I slipped back out of the garden, left the building and began walking away fast. For some reason, as I walked, I started thinking about the house I'd grown up in, in Seattle, the little yard, playing out there on the swings. I was a nice girl, a good girl. Had always been. There was no way to explain what I had just done. Coercion? But I hadn't been coerced. Brainwashed, colonized? I imagined a court case here in Buenos Aires. Next I saw the look of bewilderment on my mother's face.

But we were just playing, I imagined telling my mother.

My age made it all the more bizarre. If I'd been twenty, it would have been different. But thirty-five? The age when you turn a corner one way or the other. What corner had I turned? Murder, incarceration. I'd be lucky if I got off with thirty, forty years. I'd be out at seventy-five. The end of my life too. The end of life.

I suddenly felt that I had to call Gabriel. Of all the people I knew here, he was the one I trusted most. I'll do whatever he says, whatever he thinks is right, I thought.

I was at home now. It was late, midnight. I called Gabriel, but there was no answer. The idea of calling Leonarda frightened me, as if it would bring me closer to the very thing I feared, as if, if I spoke to her, the worst would be confirmed.

I called Gabriel again. No answer.

I spent a horrific night. Wide awake, imagining things. When I did sleep, for forty-five minutes or so, I dreamed again of my childhood backyard.

In the morning, Gabriel called me back. I asked him to come over right away.

"What is it?"

"Please just come. I can't tell you on the phone."

It took a while, but I was happy to have something precise to wait for. Rather than something horrific but imprecise, looming. Finally, he arrived.

"What happened?" he asked as soon as I opened the door.

I brought him inside. I was speaking rapidly, at first in a very soft voice, so no one could hear. Even though the building, as both he and I knew, had some of the thickest walls in the world.

"Wait, I can't hear you," he said. "Speak up."

I told him the whole story. Halfway through, I started to cry.

When I'd finished, Gabriel's face looked crushed. "I never trusted that girl," he said.

This made me start crying harder.

"But wait, wait," he said, pulling himself together. "I'm not saying I believe the guy's dead. Take it easy." He stood up.

"But the smell—"

"Maybe the smell's from something else. If he's dead, it would've been in the news."

"But they haven't found him yet," I said. "That's why there's the smell."

"Just take it easy. Have you checked the news?"

I hadn't.

"Let me do that now."

He went to my computer. There was no Wi-Fi set up in the apartment, but sometimes if you went near the window you could pick up a signal.

I was sitting down on the floor, huddled into a ball.

"I can't get a signal," he said, after a few minutes of holding my computer up near the windows. "Have you spoken to Leonarda?"

I shook my head.

"Why don't you call her? Maybe she knows something. Maybe she's even seen him since."

I got up and found my phone. Instinctively, I'd wanted to keep my distance from Leonarda. But I was determined to do what Gabriel told me. I called.

The phone rang and rang. No answer.

"No answer," I said, putting it down.

In the meantime, Gabriel had received a call. "Okay, okay, I'm leaving in a minute," he said, exasperated, to whomever it was.

"Listen," he now said to me. "I have to do a delivery, out to the suburbs. Then I'll come back. It should take me a few hours, no more than that. Just try to relax. Anything could've happened. Maybe he went out of town. The guy travels a lot. He left some food rotting. Or the sewer system's out."

Once he was gone, I tried Leonarda again. I called and called her.

This had never happened, that I'd called this much and she hadn't answered. I interpreted it as a terrible sign. She'd been caught. Or worse, and more likely, she'd disappeared, was leaving me to shoulder all the blame.

I checked my watch. Only a half an hour had passed since Gabriel had left. There was no way in hell I could wait here for hours.

I decided to go over to Miguel's again. Action, I had to take action.

I took a taxi. Again, I pictured police cars crowded together outside The Palace of Pigeons. Again, they weren't there. I didn't recognize the doorman on duty. He was young, must've been new. I said I was going to see Miguel. The indoor pillars, the polished floor. Again, I rang the bell.

There was silence for a moment, then a sound. A moment later, Miguel opened the door.

"Oh!" I said. I flushed. I was stammering. I could never have predicted being so happy to see him. He was wearing shorts, socks. "Please excuse me," he said. I knew he didn't like to be seen in shorts and socks. While this had struck me as ridiculous before, now it seemed touching. He returned a moment later, changed into long pants.

He bowed and invited me in.

"So—you're all right?" I asked, still stammering.

"Yes, of course." He smiled. Was it a smirk? I didn't care, I was so relieved. "Would you like a drink?" he asked, though it was just twelve noon.

"Sure," I said. A drink sounded good.

He was already heading toward the kitchen. I looked around.

Even his house seemed dear to me in this moment. It had been tidied, everything in its place.

He returned with a bottle of grappa, two small glasses. He poured us each a glass and sat down at his desk chair.

"How's your research project going?" he asked.

"Fine," I said. "I'm actually just writing up my report."

I took a sip of grappa. I couldn't tell if it was the drink or just relief, this feeling of pleasure infusing my limbs.

"And your book?" I asked. He was at work on a new book.

"Fine, fine."

"Will you be traveling to the States soon?" I knew that he'd been invited to appear on a panel at the University of Texas, Austin.

"In a month's time."

"How long will you stay?"

"Not so long. Two and a half weeks."

He served us each another finger of grappa.

We talked about American writers, their propensity to drink, the tradition of alcohol in American letters. We talked about newspapers.

"I only read *The New York Times* for the sports," he said.

It was the conversation we might have had in the beginning, if we'd met under different circumstances.

As he sat there sipping his drink, almost ostentatiously dignified, he had a kind of melancholy about him that made me think of death. Not imminent death—that had been mercifully avoided—but eventual, inevitable death. The creature dies in the end. The anxiety of this is what makes him behave in any kind of crazy way, to make himself forget, avoid the thought.

It hadn't been there at first, but now I caught a vague whiff of the strange, rotten smell. My horror must have exaggerated it the night before. Still it was there. The creature dies in the end. But this was not the end. Far from it. In fact, more than anything, he seemed amused.

I'm amusing him, I thought. And, gradually, as my relief wore off, I began to feel ridiculous.

From the start, it had been clear that I lacked their sophistication, their grandiose imagination. But now I felt confronted even more blatantly by my American earnestness. I had actually thought that we had killed him. I'd pictured being on trial, locked up for murder. I remembered the other times I'd gotten frightened or outraged in the course of our encounters, like that day I'd stood up and left in a panic. All at once, everything seemed clear to me. My credulity had been essential to their amusement. After the last incident, Leonarda had probably just returned and untied him. They'd had a drink, laughed.

Suddenly, I felt the need to leave. Again, we engaged in our peculiar bowing ritual at the door.

"I'm glad to see you looking so well," I said.

"Likewise," he answered.

As soon as I was back on the street again, I called Leonarda. She picked up.

"Where have you been?" I asked.

"On a secret journey," she said. "To the heart of the U.S. security system."

I didn't care what she was talking about. "Listen, I have to talk to you. Where are you?"

"In a car." This was also new. She was never in a car. "I can be dropped off wherever you are. Where are you?"

"By the zoo."

"Okay, I'll meet you in ten minutes in front of the zoo."

I waited. The zoo entrance was on a large roundabout. The car, whoever's car it was, must have dropped her off on the far side. She came running across the street, an iPod in her ears.

"Listen," I said, "I want you to tell me clearly. What the fuck was that whole thing with Miguel?"

"What whole thing?" she asked, pulling the iPod out of her ears.

"That whole . . . thing. I just had a total freak-out. I thought we'd killed him, left him to die, tied up there."

"Oh—" She was covering her mouth with her hand, laughing. "You're adorable."

"Okay, Leonarda, stop with that." I looked away. The elephants behind us were making noises.

"Should we go take a look at them?" Leonarda asked, craning her neck to see the elephants.

"No," I answered. "Listen, I just went to see him, Miguel, to check, make sure he was okay. Now I feel like you were both laughing at me that whole time. There was nothing genuine—"

She interrupted me. "Oh, yes, it was genuine. It was beautiful, the way the whole plan unfolded." She sounded rapturous. She also sounded like she was talking about something in the distant past.

I insisted on a question I had asked before. "And what was I in that plan?"

"You were perfect."

"What do you mean, I was the perfect plaything?" I said it angrily, bitterly.

"No, no. You were always perfect." Now she even looked like she had tears in her eyes. "You didn't disappoint me. That rarely happens."

I went home and lay down on the floor, those words ringing in my mind. I hadn't disappointed her, whatever that meant. It was certainly a mixed compliment, but one that I felt too bewildered at the moment to understand. Later, I would have to go through and rethink everything. But now I needed to rest. I lay there, heart jumping, blood coursing in my veins, alive, unquestionably alive, if entirely unmoored.

thirty-one

Six months later, I was in the Boedo neighborhood again. I passed under a eucalyptus tree, tore some leaves off, crushed them, smelled them. Water was running out from under a closed door. I walked by, backed up, looked again. It rippled out onto the sidewalk, clear water. Thoughts or things I'd heard would float through my brain. We are living in the torrential present, water running under a door.

I had decided to stay on. The botanist had written me. He wanted me to do some research for him about the Argentine water hyacinth, one of the most notorious invasive plant species on the planet. Its reach was wide. It was currently causing major havoc in waterways in Africa, Asia and Australia, as well as the southern United States. A new effort was being launched to find a biological control agent to stem its growth. I could be part of it. He'd hooked me up with a lab.

"Good," Gabriel had said when I told him. "Further study of the natives." He flashed his demon smile.

"What about you?" I asked. "How are you doing?"

"Okay, though a weird thing's happening. I'm just not that interested in sex these days."

"Really?"

"Yeah. I mean, I have a meeting with a client and then I just don't feel like going. I've been thinking about medicine. I want to start studying again."

I smiled. "'Eros is life'?" I asked.

"Yeah, well, I'm beginning to think maybe it's just a part of life."

Isolde had stopped working at the beauty parlor, moved in with Hernán and was expecting a child. I had just been out to see Vera. The territory on the far side of the river where the beauty parlor was had historically been considered outside the law. If you got in trouble in Buenos Aires, you could always gather your belongings, cross the bridge and disappear there. But when I arrived at the hairdresser's, it was Vera who had gone.

"She just picked up the other day and got on a bus," the owner, Juana, said. "She didn't tell anyone where she was going."

As I got waxed and had my toes done by a new woman, I kept returning to an image of Vera, sitting there alone on the bus. What could she be thinking? Her children had grown. She was setting out again on her own, writing for herself a secret history. In that moment, this history of hers seemed as precious to me as the histories of any of the great conquerors or queens.

Now I was on my way to an opening. It was in an upstairs gallery, a new place. Up ahead I saw figures I recognized, surely also on their way there. Downstairs from the gallery, the woman with the red hair and tilted head was locking her bike up to a tree. The steps inside were steep.

A little while later, I was ready to leave. I'd looked at the photos, had a few glasses of wine out on the terrace, talked to some people.

Then I saw her, Leonarda, in a new guise, her hair up bouffant style. She had her glasses on and a deep fuchsia Sophia Loren–style dress. I hadn't seen her for over four months, though I'd heard that she'd gotten married to the famous, shy hacker and had started singing cabaret. I had been planning on dropping by one of her shows.

She was talking to the skydiver we'd met that time together at the nerd bar, the hacker, her new husband, standing on her other side. I looked closely at the hacker. Was he prey? Her hand was placed sweetly on his arm. Had she actually fallen in love? It was certainly possible. The one dependable thing about her was that she would change.

I had come up a few paces behind them with every intention of saying hello, but found myself pausing for a second to listen.

"I guess you're too evolved for that, right?" the skydiver was saying. "You've evolved so far into the future?"

Leonarda looked at him. "I'm not evolved. I *am* the future. I'm, like, post-human."

A moment later, out on the street again, for no discernible reason, I felt myself invaded by a strange sort of happiness.

The sensitized streetlamps going on one by one. I walked along. Sometimes the street names were placed on the corners of the buildings, sometimes not. A dog paused, arched its back. There was graffiti on the walls. "To choose is to age." Who said that? Who cares? I pictured myself taking a right, then a left, then a right again.

acknowledgments

I'm grateful to readers Mary Gordan, Jin Auh, Alfredo Grieco, Jane Brodie, Bliss Broyard, Wendy Gosselin, Aoibheann Sweeney and Sarah McGrath; to the following people for conversations that helped illuminate the book, Nadia Tomchyshyna, Mauricio Corbalán, Ryan Tracy, Silke Bayer, Fundación Start, Marisela La Grave, Heather Goodwind, Luis Pérez, Samuel Arrues; to Yaddo and the Dora Maar House for artistic sanctuary; and, above all, to Martín Sivak.

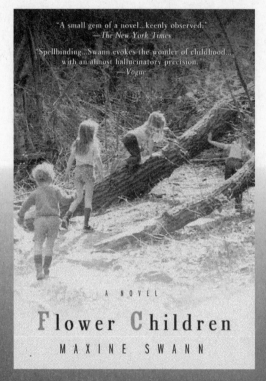